ROWAN BLAIZE

BOOK ONE OF THE ENCHANTED HERITAGE CHRONICLES

BY JONATHAN KIERAN

Published in the United States by Brightbourne Media

© 2012 Jonathan Kieran
Brightbourne Media

www.rowanblaize.com

Library of Congress Cataloguing in Publication Data applied for

ISBN-10: 0615708730

ISBN-13: 9780615708737

Rowan Blaize

BOOK ONE OF THE ENCHANTED HERITAGE CHRONICLES

I

Of Peril Amid the Tempest

Within a maelstrom twisted, coiling,
clouds of stinging ice were boiling,
Surging up with howling screams
of desperate Wind Gods loosed-by-dreams;
from visions sped through darkest portals,
shadows cast by mad immortals.
I—yes, I!—was trapped and lost,
upon a vengeful tempest tossed.

What farce that I, a son of Powers
spawned at Time's beginning,
the progeny of unseen realms
by common storm sent spinning!

For I have lived two thousand years
and then eight hundred more.
I have, by magic, navigated
firmament and shore.

Yes, mountain peak and black abyss
by sorcery I've seen,
and like a thread-through-needle
have explored worlds in-between.

All through this web of centuries
I've taken many forms,
but *never* in that maze of years
have failed to conquer storms!

At need I have appeared to be
the glimmer in a jewel.
For other tricks I cloaked myself
as king, as bard, as fool.

Though strains of mortal kinship
now seem shrouded in the mist,
with mortals We are bound
and find it wise to co-exist.

To ravages of time and tide
my kind are quite immune,
while human folk like mayflies come,
then wither swift and soon.

Disease has never pestered us,
though sadness we can feel.
In fact, from mortal lovelorn scenes
we *have* been known to steal.

Yet otherwise we glide through time
untroubled by the hours …
unless perchance we're hobbled
by the loss of all our powers!

For many reasons this affliction
comes to such as We.
Ironic that, with foresight's aid,
these blights we fail to see.

This thundercloud of turbulence,
its blasts and swoops and swells,
had caught me unaware and—worse—
bereft of all my spells.

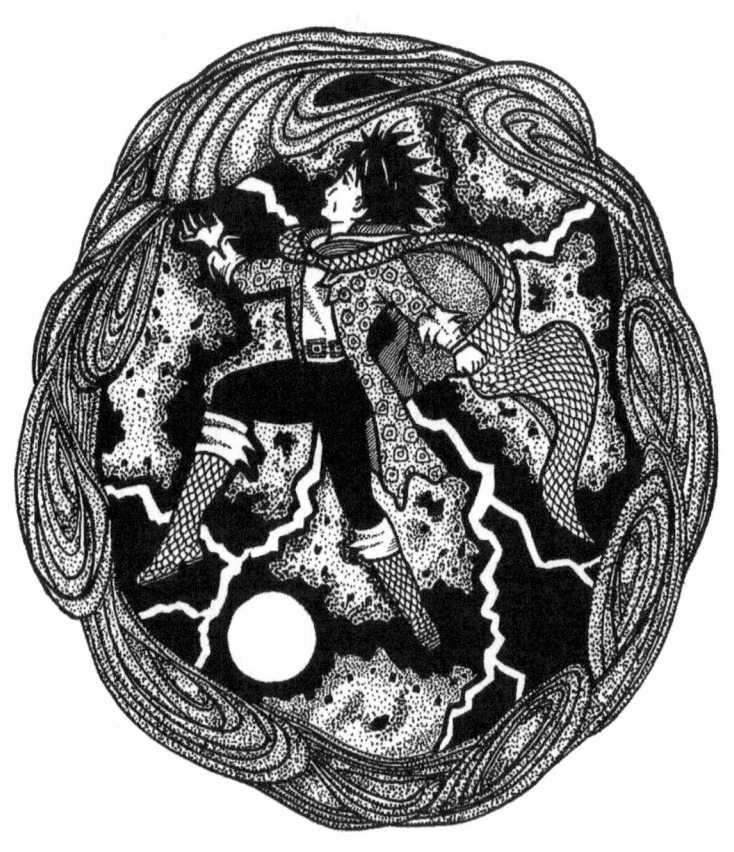

Some words of power, six in all,
I voiced, though hoarse and thin.
Yet not the ablest spirit
seemed to hear me through the din.

No time to guess or ponder how
this peril came to plague me,
for in a brilliant lightning flash
I glimpsed some treetops, vaguely.

"At least," I thought while dangling
on the brink of my despair,
"There's half a chance I *might* survive
this circus in the air."

Those trees indeed had spurred some hope
while thunder boomed around.
"If I can aim for branch or limb,
I might not hit the ground!"

For though our forms are stronger
than are those of mortal birth,
without our magic we *can* die
if smashed against the earth.

"Krestohk! Feerlahk! Vohss!" I cried,
in one last vain attempt
to stave-off certain dooms from which
I'm normally exempt.

But magic failed and on the pelting
hailstones I did choke.
The storm next spit me out
and then I crashed into an oak.

II

A Host Most Unexpected

A mammoth tree of ancient days
amid the bluster swings and sways.
Its branches scraped, its leaves did scratch,
and deigned my hurtling form to catch.
Then plucking me from Zephyr's powers,
it lodged me twixt two saving bowers.
Rains that pummeled, rife with brawn,
soon ceased their rage; the storm moved on.

Imagine one in shame suspended,
dazed and most confused,
by jutting limbs now skewered,
and by impact sorely bruised.

Upside-down I hung like Odin
—not a rune in sight.
A windblown piece of random trash
as dusk bowed toward the night.

Indeed the evening lurked along
an edge of Eastern sky.
One peek through tangled darkness—Lo!
A farmhouse I did spy.

Before my addled brain gave thought
to how I might descend,
the branches cracked, the limbs gave way,
and bounced me end-to-end.

Here a thud! and there a bump!
with thrashing all around.
I lost my perch atop the oak
and finally hit the ground.

What breath I had recovered
once the maelstrom set me free,
was pounded from my weary lungs
amid the soaked debris.

Fortuna is a thankless wretch
(I've met her and should know)
and even Sons of Magic guess
not how her wheel might go.

Thus in the fallout of my plight
and powers helter-skelter,
I had no recourse but to find
the nearest, safest, shelter.

On shaking legs I struggled,
sliding up against the oak.
Across the twilight meadow,
farmhouse chimneys spewed their smoke.

I looked about and gathered wits
and wondered where I'd landed.
On sleepy English countryside,
'twas clear I had been stranded.

"How *could* he know this, void of Power?"
the reader might inquire.
But I was soaring, London-bound,
when power did expire.

Although I had survived the fray
with naught but few abrasions,
I've known an English countryside
on countless fine occasions.

I have a vibrant history on the land
where I stood, grounded,
for on this island I was born
when Rome was being founded.

My leather coat was tattered
and my trollskin boots were wrinkled.
Throughout my sopping, tangled hair
some oak tree leaves were sprinkled.

My nose was bleeding slightly
but I sensed no wound internal,
and slid a sleeve across my face
while cursing Luck infernal.

In truth I was not justified
in muttering a curse.
As plunges from the heavens go,
things could have gone much worse.

Then straightening my shoulders
I began to weave a spell.
Perhaps the storm alone
had robbed my strength—I couldn't tell.

Alas, instead of feeling
that familiar take-off "lift,"
I felt a chill pierce through me
as the dreary wind did shift.

No doubt remained within me:
all my witching strength had died.
As darkness waxed I looked about
For some place I could hide.

The little English farmhouse
with its windows softly lit,
might seem, to some, a haven
but for me 'twas hardly fit.

Do not mistake my words
for, in the past, in many nations,
I've been in circumstances boasting
worse accommodations.

A sorcerer who's lost the power
to make his cauldron bubble,
when stranded in the mortal world
is rarely far from trouble.

In ancient times the human race
took care to welcome strangers—
a practice long-since buried
'neath an avalanche of dangers.

Nor would the nearby forest be
a better choice of lodging.
Ten times as grave would be
the certain perils I'd be dodging.

I braced myself against the oak
and searched the rising gloom
for some old barn or crumbling shed
that might afford me room.

And just when I had settled
on a paddock stacked with hay,
I heard a low and surly voice
behind me growl and say:

"Unless you want a knock, my lad,
You'll turn around *real* slow."
My instinct was to dash,
but who could say how far I'd go?

My legs were quite uncertain
and my mind a tad afloat.
But all the same I steeled my nerves
and smoothed my ruined coat.

When caught off-guard by mortals
one is faced with many choices.
When stripped of all one's power
it is best to heed their voices.

Composed as I could be,
I looked away from yonder hovel.
And turning on my heel I saw
a toad-like man (with shovel).

"Good sir, let me assure you,
as the rain streaks from my brow.
I did not mean to trespass
and intend to cause no row."

But the shovel-wielding elder,
with his face all warts and spots,
just blinked and moved across the oak tree's
sprawled and rooty knots.

"You're not from round these parts, my boy,
I see that from your clothes.
You're not one of McHale's young lads.
You ain't no son of Joe's.

"When I first saw you standing here,
as I was heading home,
I thought for sure you was a kid
from down Mad Ramble's Roam.

"Them folk are always messing
round my place by day and night.
A-thinking they can make a fool
of me and cause a fright.

"But you ain't one of that lot,
I can see it plain as plain.
'Cause even *those* fools ain't so daft
to stand out in the rain."

To this appraisal I had not
a great deal I could add.
"In storm and rain I stand, Good Sir,
but *you* stand *with* this lad."

The codger shrugged and said,
"Tis true, but least I got a reason.
This farm is mine and one must work
no matter what the season.

"The storm knocked down a sapling
that I planted just today.
I grabbed me shovel, coat, and cap
and went about me way."

With stubby thumb he indicated
some spot near an orchard.
'Twas where he'd likely bury me
As soon as I'd been tortured!

"But no more talk of *me,* young man,
this ain't about my chores.
I'm owed an explanation why
you lurk in my outdoors!"

"The tale is rather lengthy, Sir,
and I feel fairly sure,
the story told in detail would be
more than you'd endure."

The toady farmer nodded.
In the distance, thunder rumbled.
He tapped his shovel on the ground
and presently he grumbled.

"You got some secret going on,
that part is crystal clear.
I *was* a lad myself once,
so you've nothing much to fear.

"I'm guessing you have run away
from home, and that's a pity.
Round here, when kids pull stunts like that,
they head straight for the city.

"But you have done the opposite,
unless I am mistaken,
and left your folks in London
for the land of cows and bacon!"

Aghast was I by *this* concoction
till the thought dawned, fleeting:
How I "looked" to Farmer Toad
was bound to be misleading.

He saw my face, my frozen grin,
and chuckled, belly bouncing.
"I knew it, lad! So why'd you run?
Your dad give you a trouncing?

"Don't be shy, you're not the first
disgruntled pup I've seen.
How old are you? No, let me guess.
Not much beyond sixteen?

"The thing that gets me here and now,
it ain't so much your trouble.
I'm more concerned with why you're
standing *here* in oak-tree rubble.

"Them clothes you wear betray
that you're a city lad, no doubt.
But where's your bag of stuff
is what I cannot figure out."

"My bag of stuff?" I parroted.
The farmer waved a hand.
"The pack of stuff *all* truants need
to travel 'cross the land!"

"I fear I must have lost that bag,"
I chattered feeling chilled.
"The storm just scooped me up, you see,
then blew me where it willed."

" 'Twas quite a blast, and no mistake,"
He whistled through his teeth.
"It cut a right destructive path
through forest, moor, and heath.

"But say no more, my boy,
it won't be known that Devon Mould
don't know enough to bring
a luckless lad in from the cold."

With that, dear Farmer Mould stomped past
in sprays of muck and mire.
"Come by the house, we'll talk a bit
while sitting near the fire."

Away we trudged across the yard
As chickens squawked and scattered.
Upon some nearby tin-roofed shack,
new raindrops popped and pattered.

Full dark had finally settled
when we entered that old house.
The place was quite unkempt
and seemed a nest fit for a mouse.

Yet, in the midst of all the pots
and piles and bits of junk,
the hearth was blazing 'Welcome'
and dispelled the Mouldy funk.

"This mess you'll have to pardon, Lad,"
he croaked with shovel down.
"Just seat yourself at fireside.
I'll have a look around.

"There's dry clothes round here somewhere,
though I won't vouch for the fit.
Some pants, a coat, perhaps a scarf.
My darling loves to knit."

"And that would be your wife?" I whispered
by the crackling flame.
"It would, indeed, my boy," he said,
"and Emma is her name."

He fixed me with a froggy eye
while riffling through some drawers.
"But don't blame *her* for this disgrace
of crammed and filthy floors.

"My Emma died nine years ago,
just slipped off in her sleep.
And I've not since had heart to give
this place its proper keep.

"That wardrobe with the vase up top
is just the way she left it.
I'd move it not an inch
if I'd the strength to even heft it.

"And over by the kitchen stove,
you'll see her biscuit tin.
I haven't had the nerve to throw it out
… or look within.

"Since Emma passed I've faded, too,
like fog does in the sun.
I gather you know what I mean.
Have *you* not lost someone?"

My heart went out to Farmer Mould.
I saw his cloven spirit.
Yet nothing I could say or do
might ever hope to cheer it.

Yet somehow, by a strange design,
this widowed soul had brought
an ancient warlock hearthside
like some butterfly he'd caught.

To tell him of my origin
would prove a grave mistake.
For mortals tend to flee from news
like *that,* as from a snake.

Or else they'll be quite smitten
and demand a "demonstration."
And that's the part where things can get
most riddled with frustration.

For those of my persuasion
aren't so swift to advertise,
and in the mortal realm prefer
to travel in disguise.

Great woe to those among us who,
by backfired spell or bane,
get caught without our magic
and are pressed to "Please explain."

There are some dreadful stories
in the history of my kind,
of firewood being gathered
and of shackles meant to bind.

With power in abundance,
we have naught to fear at all,
and with an incantation
can dispel mobs great and small.

This brokenhearted farmer,
as he pined for his dead love,
reminded me of troubles
I need *not* be thinking of.

For though I'd never "lost someone"
the way he did presume,
I had a distant cousin, once,
who met an end in gloom.

Five hundred years before, I think,
(Or maybe it was six?)
a mage I knew did battle
with a warlock they called "Blix."

It was a frightful drama
and, by all reports, the mage
was soundly thrashed and trapped
within some ectoplasmic cage.

This happened in the Balkans,
where the local humans failed
to find much use for sorcerers
except when they're impaled.

So this poor dolt, my cousin,
when the fight at last was done,
discovered he was powerless
and took off on-the-run.

With mirthless Balkan gentry
he tried very hard to blend.
But when they saw he had eight eyes
they torched him in the end.

His story *does* exemplify
the problems we can face;
my family rarely speaks of it at all,
for the disgrace.

"Aha!" said Farmer Mould
who brandished in his calloused claws,
a musty woolen sweater
and some mittens for my paws.

"Here's just the thing to get you warm,
so doff those duds and change.
They're soaking wet and, might I add,
the style is *rather* strange.

"And what, pray, were you thinking, Lad?
I caught you lost in thought.
You're bound to be quite famished;
let me see what food I've got.

"No need for food, Good Sir," I said.
"My stomach's full from lunch.
I've put you out enough already.
Really—thanks a bunch."

"Nonsense, whippersnapper,
and you must not call me 'Sir,'
though niceties in one so young
these days do rare occur."

I did his will and changed my ruined
outfit as he searched
the kitchen for some tea leaves,
then back in the room he lurched.

"You must be feeling better
in that sweater and those britches."
Then picking up my boots, he frowned
and said, "What *frightful* stitches!"

"I've not seen leather quite this type
and *my* best friend's a tanner.
The texture is all pitted in such
bristly, hairy manner!"

"Those boots are made in special shops,"
I ventured to explain.
"The leather is most rare
and gets all wrinkled in the rain."

"Well, we shall put them by the fire
along with your weird jacket.
I swear those London fashion stores
are truly quite the racket.

"Seat yourself in Emma's chair,
for tea will soon be ready.
You're looking better than you did,
but seem a tad unsteady."

"How far are we from London, Sir,"
I asked as I sat down.
To this my host responded
with another puzzled frown.

"But surely you should know, my boy.
Did you not hear me say,
I'd guessed you was from London
Cos' you are a run-away?"

"The thing is much more complicated, Sir,
if you must know.
I didn't run away,
but it's to London I must *go.* "

Farmer Mould retrieved the tea
and poured a steaming cup.
"I'm one to mind my business, lad.
You need not say what's up.

"So long as you don't rob me blind
or mind that space is tight,
you're welcome to the guest room
and are free to spend the night.

"If truly you have lost your way,
and storms *do* have a knack
for blowing people far off course,
then I can help you back.

"We're only twenty miles away
From London loud and gritty.
By daylight one can even see
the skyline of the city.

"Tomorrow, when you're all dried out,
I'll put you on a bus.
The ride is not an hour's length
and minimal the fuss.

"I'd take you there myself, of course,
but sold my car last year.
I lost all love for driving
when in May I hit a deer.

"Besides, I'm old, and lately
don't remember things I should,
Supplies I get in town
and all the walking does me good."

"You're very kind, O Devon Mould.
This will not be forgotten.
But I'll not take a bus, although
I'm feeling rather rotten.

"The nearest road will suit me.
I can walk by light of day,
if in the morning you would be
so kind to point the way."

"It's all the same to me, young man,
if walking you prefer.
But till you've eaten breakfast
I shall *never* let you stir."

"Good farmer, that's a bargain.
I'd be proud to share your table.
And rest assured that one day
I'll repay … if I am able."

Devon Mould just chortled
as he slurped a bit of tea.
"Don't think about repayment, Lad,
but hearken unto me.

"Whatever set you on your run,
what ill your parents did,
have mercy and forgive them,
mad with worry for their kid!

"It always pained me deeply
that my most beloved wife
could never bear us children,
that we never "made" a life.

"Some say that's God's decision,
that His wisdom must be praised.
And anyhow my Emma brought me
joy throughout my days.

"We always had each other—
how these rooms would ring with laughter!
But since she died each day I pray
That *I* might follow after."

The farmer pointed to a wall
of photographs askance.
"You see the one on top, my lad?
That's us at some old dance.

"And over there's my favorite,
one of Emma on our porch.
You ever seen a sweeter smile?
It blazes like a torch.

"Despite the wondrous happiness
I feel to see that face,
the photo brings me heartache
'cos one thing is out of place.

"My darling lady's there in youth
and, too, the house I built.
But I'm not in the picture
and that fact fills me with guilt.

"If I could travel back in time,
through stolen years I'd flounder.
I'd have that picture taken
with me *in* it, arms around her!"

Again my heart was moved for him,
I felt his mortal grief,
since Time, for human beings,
is a most relentless thief.

"She's beautiful, your Emma,
and her light still strong and true.
The power of her kindness shines
in everything you do."

"That's mighty nice to say, my boy,
You're wiser than your years.
I hope you never have to suffer
Through *these* kinds of tears.

"For though her shadow lives in me,
A shadow's all I know.
I don't believe I'll see her
when it comes my time to go."

I sipped my warming tea and gazed
around the little place.
Each trinket was a talisman,
each nook some sacred space.

"Now don't despair, good farmer,
and beware of being certain.
For there is more than you suspect
behind life's Final Curtain."

"I hope you're right, my rain-soaked lad,
my storm-sent young intruder."
He poured more tea and tipped his pot
of tiny, tarnished pewter.

He yawned so wide and long I saw
each tooth left in his head.
Soon shadows grew, the fire died,
and time had come for bed.

"I'll show you to the spare room, now,
and trust you'll get some sleep.
Tomorrow after breakfast
off to London you shall creep."

He led me from the room
and gently straightened Emma's frame.
Then, halting in his tracks, said, "Lad!
I don't yet know your *name!*"

"While lodged beneath your roof, my friend,
as thanks from he who stays …
It's nice to meet you, Devon Mould.
My name is Rowan Blaize."

III

Afoot, Forlorn, in Trollskin Boots

At dawn's emergence, clean, renewed,
with mist the countryside endued,
and fog that probed with wraith-like fingers,
I, in haste, not keen to linger
bid my farmer host farewell,
his escort welcomed through the dell.
The night passed well, despite the trauma;
roadways new betokened drama.

"Why you won't take a bus is mad,"
croaked Farmer Mould, perplexed.
"But if you spurn this basket, Lad,
I promise to be vexed.

"I've wrapped you up some country ham
and biscuits for the walk.
There's also three boiled eggs, and best,
a thermos filled with stock."

"Most humbled by your graciousness,"
I said and took his gift.
"But in those city clothes," he huffed,
"you'll *never* get a lift."

My trollskin boots were fairly dry,
but coat of widow's silk,
and trousers made of dragon-scale
smelled sour as curdled milk.

"I'd be too claustrophobic
on a bus-ride, I confess.
And hitching lifts from strangers
is a gamble, more or less.

"But walking in the open air
is just the proper tonic.
The sounds of nature to my eager ears
will be symphonic."

"Well, mind you keep upon the road;
no detours take, for instance.
And if you feel you're getting lost,
there's London in the distance."

Indeed he gestured widely
and, not far off, through the mist,
I saw dear London's outline
then, with triumph, clenched a fist.

Though magically still useless,
smelling faint of farmhouse musk,
I guessed that I could reach the city
sometime close to dusk.

Oh, once within great London's arms
I'd make my stealthy way!
To my Aunt Ariadne's house
a visit I would pay.

"Now mind you watch for motorists,
for I remember well,
that folks in these parts tend to race
like bats that come from hell."

"I've seen such bats and they're no joke,"
I muttered 'neath my breath.
"I swear that I'll be careful, friend,"
and then 'twas when I left.

"How grand to have your company!
Now make your way back home.
And be on guard when you should pass
by Old Mad Ramble's Roam.

"It's one thick patch of forest
and the road's all hairpin turns.
You'll have to walk the ditch
or get plowed down amid the ferns!"

"Much thanks to share your shelter,
you've been gracious with your trust.
And I shall keep in mind
Each crucial thing we have discussed.

"But more than even safety
I appreciate the gift
of tales of your dear Emma,
and I pray your spirits lift.

"I'll not forget your candor,
nor your willingness to speak
of matters rooted in the heart,
of memories grand and bleak.

"For now I can repay you
only with a stranger's blessing.
Henceforth your days be peaceful
and the long nights less distressing!

"I bid at last, dear farmer,
that my thanks with you remain.
Do not forget this wayward soul
you rescued from the rain."

The fog was undulating
as I shook the farmer's hand
and ambled down the Sutton road,
to walk the waiting land.

With new determination and
a stately, forceful stride,
I launched upon that roadway
into mists that swirled beside.

My legs not used to walking much,
I'd only gone a mile,
when out of breath I deemed it wise
to pause a little while.

That morning I had tried a spell
(or two) to test my strength.
With power not forthcoming
I soon gave it up at length.

I'd faked the rite of breakfast
for, to us, a mortal's food
is mostly unappealing,
though it's far worse to be rude.

The basket I'd been given
at my side did swing and sway,
but such a gracious gift I had
no heart to toss away.

I hated feeling weakened
and above all did despise
that reasons for my power-loss
I *still* could not surmise.

I pined for some ambrosia,
just a glass to calm my nerves.
A bowl of satyr's milk is what
a sickened mage deserves!

My dear Aunt Ariadne
could provide me with such fare.
But first I had to brace myself
and get from here to *there.*

Continuing the journey though
the land with fog was clotted,
I gazed upon the region which
with cozy homes was dotted.

Thus envying the mortals safe
and sound within each dwelling,
I hoped my Aunt was even *home* in London;
there's no telling.

That's because my Auntie
gets around, despite her age.
She shifts at will from world to world,
her whims most hard to gauge.

Yet no one else in London
could I trust to help me guess
exactly how or why I'd gotten
into this fine mess.

So on I trudged the waxing morn
and twice was forced to dash
when honking cars sped by me
and through shallow puddles splashed.

One fine mortal driver
from his window deigned to speak:
"Get out the way, you foolish, daft,
and MEASLY city freak!"

In fairness I was in the road,
but thought I was alone.
Aye, if I'd had my powers
I'd have turned his car to stone!

My mood did not improve much
even when the sun emerged.
Upon a time I, too, could part the clouds;
I felt submerged.

This suburb of the city
I could not too well recall.
It *had* been generations
since I'd passed this spot at all.

The bulk of all past visits
were confined to London proper,
though Mother used to tour the forests;
no one *dared* to stop her.

Moreover, when in England,
all my journeys are by air.
This stratosphere the "highway"
that can take me anywhere.

Don't want to make it seem as though
I've *never* used a road.
At many times in life
I sought to lighten magic's load.

But note the stunning difference
when this thing is done for sport,
or exploits of the self-intriguing,
entertaining sort.

All mortal folksy annals
are replete with gripping tales
of magical encounters on
the grandest, greatest scales.

Why, I myself, one heady month
in ancient Samarkand,
transformed myself into a flautist
with a travelling band.

We played for wine-drunk lords
and for the poor on city streets.
Each night by roaring bonfires danced
for all we chanced to meet.

Enchantments I did weave through
every tune and piping note,
so all who heard our music found
a lump come to the throat.

Such magic noises lingered long
in captivated heads,
and caused them dreams so vivid
they would fly straight from their beds!

'Twas all a bit of mischief wrought
to tweak the mortal mind.
A casual diversion from
those spells of graver kind.

Yet tricks of such insouciance
are never done at need.
Wild games are played when one
can craft escape at lightning speed.

Upon the lonesome country road
that moment in my plight,
I wondered if I'd reach the city's
outskirts by the night.

Adding apprehension
as the morning hours waned,
a drooping tuft of storm-cloud moved
o'erhead—again, it rained.

My garb still moist from yesterday,
my patience nigh depleted,
I clutched the farmer's basket
and to nearby woods retreated.

This new downpour was nothing like
the cyclone one night prior,
but pelting drops gave chase
as I plowed madly through the briar.

Once beneath a thicket I peered out
to see the cloud,
my coat bedecked with thistles
like some parasitic shroud.

No sign of break was imminent,
the heavens sagged with grey.
It rained the kind of rain it rains
when rainclouds mean to stay.

Through windy waves of bristling sheets
I scanned the scene in vain
and spotted past the ditch a sign
that spelled out "Croydon Lane."

There was no point in setting out
until the weather calmed.
The blood beneath my skin was chilled
as if with ice embalmed.

Behind the roadside forest
sprawled a dense and darkling grove.
I shuffled through the leafy wet,
'twas deep the path I wove.

The canopy above afforded
here-and-there protection.
In minutes I had lost all sense
of purpose and direction.

Whatever foul affliction
had deprived me of my power,
I knew that it might *finish* me
within that fateful hour.

Another rugged oak I came to
as I slipped and slunk.
Without a thought I climbed
and wedged my body in its trunk.

"The madness and the irony!"
I wanted then to shout.
"Today I'm climbing *up* a tree …
Last night was tumbling out!"

I clutched the farmer's basket
and was tempted to partake
of something he had packed for me
but could not stay awake.

The raindrops filtered through the limbs
above on whistling breeze.
"Morpheus!" I cursed
and fell asleep with head-on-knees.

IV
A Muddle of Minions Meddlesome

Images of cities tumbling:
bastions; ramparts; archways crumbling.
Time and War all signs unheeded,
scepters smashed, their kings defeated.
Thousands surge in shadowed shape,
upon their lips one cry—"Escape!"
Behold the waiting Sea of Tears.
They plunge from cliffs, beset by spears …

The dream that clutched my waking mind
like smoke in wind dispelled.
'Twas not by crushing ruins
but with *hands* that I was felled!

"Knock him down and search him now!"
a hundred voices wailed.
I tried to grab a branch and swat them off—
alas, I failed.

"His coat is full of thistles, boys!
Watch out or you'll get stuck.
By Mab, these boots are trollskin!
How is *that* for faery luck?"

"Remove your hands at once from me,"
I muttered in the dark.
"Not wise to wake a sorcerer
who's sleeping in the park."

"And pray what kind of sorcerer,"
one wheedling voice began,
"goes napping in a tree-trunk like
some drunken mortal man?"

"I'll take no cheek from the likes of you,
nor any in your crowd!
A warlock sleeps wherever
and waits not to be allowed."

This bravery meant nothing
for I was, in fact, surrounded
by a gang of wretched woodland sprite:
How earnestly they hounded!

The night had plainly fallen
but I did not know the hour.
Assaulted by these rabble fey,
I rued my lack of power.

At least two hundred of them swarmed,
the size of gecko lizards.
Sapphire eyes were sparkling like
the crystal runes of wizards.

What grave miscalculation
to have wandered from the road!
With laughter each fey mocked me
as their skin in moonlight glowed.

They grabbed my hair in handfuls
and they dragged me from the tree.
I landed on my rump and hoped
I'd squashed one, two, or three.

But faery folk are swift as wind,
so out of reach they scattered.
Once they bound my hands with vine
no fit or tantrum mattered.

"Enough, you little insects!
From these revelries desist.
I had no clue that in these woods
A fey tribe might exist."

"That's *your* misfortune, Sleepy,"
said one clamped upon my collar.
"To know the mere potential, friend,
does not require a scholar."

"Please listen," I protested
as they wrapped me up in cords.
"I thought you'd long died-out round here,
much less survived in hordes!"

A frightful din of catcalls echoed
through the ferny dell.
"How like a snobby warlock to assume
we'd gone to hell!

"We saw you sneaking in our wood,"
one added with a glare.
"We guessed you was a sorcerer
whose powers are threadbare.

"Just look at your condition, Sir,
Your clothes is wet and ripped!
No wizard worth his wand would walk
around like *that,*" he quipped.

"It's true that I am ill just now,
no other way to spin it.
But rest assured my powers *will*
come back at any minute.

"And when they do you may expect
a rather grand display
of magic that will turn you all
to bits of molding clay.

"And when you've been transformed
I'll take each lump that has offended,
then put them on a potter's wheel
till all your bits are blended!

"I'll probe and shape that messy blob
until at last I've got
an object fitting for the kiln
—a faery chamber pot!"

Each sprite let out an angry gasp;
their pride I had insulted.
I thought the threat might sway their plans
but no such thing resulted.

Instead, their cheeky "leader,"
who was camped on my lapel,
said, "Drag him to the King, my lads.
He's got no hex or spell."

A mob on the periphery
were mad as ants to see
what loomed in Farmer's basket
as it leaned against the tree.

"Behold and be astonished, friends,
and gather round, my brothers!
This basket's full of mortal treats,
like cheese and several others."

One fey sliced the country ham
to brandish on his knife.
"A chance to eat some piggie, lads.
By Mab, don't tell me wife!"

Two more grabbed the thermos top
and strained till it came loose.
Then sniffing in, they gave a grin:
"Great gods, it's CHICKEN JUICE!"

"You have no right to pilfer there,"
I snapped while being dragged.
"And *you* no power to stop us, Sir,"
the faery captain bragged.

Now tightly bound and helpless
in the noisy, teeming mass,
I struggled as they heaved me ho
through rock and dirt and grass.

I could not place this breed of fey
(there are so many tribes)
but noticed how stick-thin they were
while listening to their jibes.

The lot of them seemed starving
and their garb far worse than mine.
Why, most were clothed in bits of moss
held up with lengths of twine.

A fool I was to even let
such Forest Folk unseat me.
Much worse would be my day
if I allowed the imps to eat me!

Such things are not unheard of,
and it *has* been known for ages
that faeries hit by famine
have a taste for stricken mages.

Most, of course, would never dare
since, even if they ate one,
a warlock's friends could take revenge …
if he had been a great one.

Diplomacy is always wise
for spirits thinking clearly.
But caution is no guarantee
when meat is craved so dearly!

"I say, you lanky specimen!
If you knew what was best,
you'd loose these bonds and treat me
like a cherished, honored guest."

The captain stood as ever and,
with most surprising haste,
his mates my body hauled across
the muddy woodland waste.

"I'll thank you to reserve remarks
for parley with the King."
The captain gestured with a twig-sized spear,
my nose to sting.

"Oh, give up all that posturing!"
I said with rolling eyes.
"We both know you won't harm me;
to your king I'll be a prize."

"That much is true," the captain huffed
as forest gloom grew thicker.
"Now, if you'll give your name
'twill make the introductions quicker!"

"As if I'd fall for that old trick,"
I scoffed beneath my captor.
"Should you be writing some bright book,
then please leave *out* that chapter.

"I know what faery folk can do,
provided with a name.
We've all toyed with that magic,
so your overture is lame."

"They really must be backward fey,"
I muttered to myself.
"To think that I'd just give my name
to such a pesky elf."

For names are rife with power,
whether common or renowned,
and all who practice magic know:
Through names are forces bound.

As word alone, a name can strike,
can punish and subdue.
A name can conjure kingdoms lost …
or wipe-out kingdoms new.

"To pass the time on this most scenic
unexpected trip,
I think I'll try to guess *your* name,"
I sneered with snaking lip.

"Jacky Peasy-Blossom, is it?
Henry Mustard Seed?
Perhaps your name is Albert
Mucky Duckling Dill-Wad Reed?"

"Oh, have your lovely laugh, my friend,
for very very soon,
when face to face with King Narzell
you'll sing a different tune!"

"Aha!" I cried as leaves and tangled branches
brushed my face,
as over bumpy ground these faeries
dragged me on apace.

My captor put his hand up to his
mouth and firmly clamped it.
He lifted up a foot and on my breast
he madly stamped it.

"You tricky little wizard!"
the frustrated faery seethed.
"It's not fair play—you know how easy
Wee Folk are deceived."

"Indeed I do, and though my spells
have sadly blown a fuse,
you gave your monarch's name.
That's an advantage I can use!"

"By Gor' we'll see," the faery whimpered
ruing his mistake.
"We're coming to the palace now …
the King my bones will break!"

Wrapped up like a mummy,
like a fly in spider strands,
I saw the poorest "palace"
I had seen in all the lands.

The puckish rout had rolled me
down a hill into a glade.
A bonfire blazed and on the edge of night
weird shadows made.

A host of rag-tag creatures lurked
within that midnight camp,
expressions tinged with misery,
some coughing in the damp.

From every nearby branch they swung
or lounged on mushroom stools.
Some peeked at me from rustic huts
or puddle swimming-pools.

The common trait to all I saw
was splendor that survived
in meager hints that proved
their noble ways no longer thrived.

From canyon pass to aerie peak
and cave where echoes ring,
of faery pomp and pageantry
the world once used to sing.

Yet Fate can be unkind to creatures
mortal *and* undying;
the fortunes of the one bound to the other
… through Time flying.

This depressed collective
was most clearly past its prime.
And yet, in every spirit lingered
signs of the sublime.

A dryad on an elm-tree stump
maintained a baleful stare.
With petulance she tossed her head
of green, disheveled hair.

Still, something in her gaze betrayed
a trace of iridescence,
a not-extinguished remnant
of some long-diminished presence.

A water nixie gazed into a mirror
near the fire.
Her saddened face was pockmarked
and her legs knee-deep in mire.

A pair of goblins shivered
as they gnawed upon a bone.
Nearby, a crippled banshee
made an unconvincing moan

One quite bedraggled griffin plucked
a flimsy, errant feather.
A werebeast of some sort was snoring
on a patch of heather.

Six or seven crylvanes formed
a circle sewing skins.
A warty hedge-witch switched
a pleading gremlin on the shins.

A triple-headed shadwock
picked its ears, all six erect.
And afterwards each finger
by the firelight did inspect.

In every quadrant of the place
some surly spirit languished.
Despite the cheerful blaze
the very air seemed cruel and anguished.

Thus I, the guest of honor in this
woeful, eldritch space,
lay bound and on my back
as shadows danced upon my face.

The captain of the fey
that caught me sleeping in the oak,
jumped down into the gully and
with haughty tones he spoke.

"Behold, me fine companions of
this palace most esteemed!
The lads and I have bagged a catch
like no one's ever dreamed."

"What is it? Is it edible?" the banshee
came and croaked.
"We cook it now?" the crylvanes wailed;
my face with spit they soaked.

"You know I don't eat white meat,"
said the nixie (few could hear her).
She whispered something else and then
looked back into her mirror.

The shadwock's fingers left its ears
and grabbed a nearby axe.
"Let's chop it into bits right now,
we're *sick* of chewing wax!"

"Now back, get back, the lot of you!
This ain't no minor thing.
We caught ourselves a sorcerer,
So go alert the king!"

Several of the creeps jumped back.
A couple even shrieked.
The banshee, lacking trademark scream,
instead let out a squeak.

"What manner of misfortune
have you brought upon us now?"
The dryad shook her leafy mane
and wrinkled-up her brow.

"We've barely got two sticks
to rub together as it stands.
What good can come from bringing
some strange warlock to our lands?"

"You've got it wrong," the faery captain
answered, looking sour.
"This fool you see before you
is a mage what's *lost his power!*"

"How can we be sure of that?"
a hag peeped round to query.
"If he's just playing possum,
things are bound to get right scary."

"Silence!" cried the faery lord.
"Don't say another thing.
We'll all know what to do ere long
for yonder comes the King!"

V

THREADBARE WAS THE MIDNIGHT KING

The bonfire roared, then seemed to fade.
Spirits scattered, room was made,
as from some secret, hidden world
a ram's horn called, a flag unfurled.
Then out of luminescent depths
a herald took four sturdy steps.
The satyr paused among the trees:
"The King is here, fools—On your knees!"

Upon a bier of ash-wood
the enthroned Narzell was carried
by four Unseeing Grimwolds
as, behind, four others tarried.

Within that gruesome coterie
that filed-out from the portal,
I spied a sullen, red-haired girl;
'twas clear she was a mortal.

The King himself with haughty gaze
surveyed the squalid scene.
His throne was chipped and battered
and his Grimwolds pale and lean.

A few more dryads clad in rags
looked ill and rather glum.
The mortal girl, to my surprise,
was chewing on some gum!

Her coat was of the puffy sort
most humans wear in weather
that's cold enough to freeze the flame
on any phoenix feather.

What sort of motley entourage
had this old King assembled?
His subjects in the glade knelt down
and to the last they trembled.

A Grimwold with the ram's horn
and a dryad with a banner
took each their proper station
in a herky-jerky manner.

The royal bier was lowered
on a mossy, flat-topped stone.
The King's attendants bowed away
and left him there alone.

I stared at him through twisting flames
and searched his grizzled face.
No fellowship I sensed in him,
no mercy—not a trace.

His robes of purple hornworm silk
were rife with shredded folds.
The fox-fur round his collar
harbored parasites untold.

His curly boots were patched with bits
of deer-hide sewn upon
the place where jewels once were fixed ...
but now those jewels were gone.

Instead of gleaming scepter,
in his hand he held a cane,
and lifted it before him,
every joint beset with pain.

"Rise, my people, from your knees!"
he rasped in sharp command.
"That, with me, you may question
this intruder to our land."

As one, the kneeling Forest Folk
obliged their Lord and King.
"Now tell me," said his Majesty.
"Who *caught* this wretched thing?"

The faery captain bowed
before the bier upon the stone,
and told of how they'd found me
in the oak—asleep, alone.

"And how did you determine
that this fellow was a mage?
Tis not a thing that every fey
is sharp enough to gauge."

"I knew it by the smell of him,"
The captain swift replied.
"I guessed it from the time I smelled
ambrosia in his hide.

"And furthermore his powers
were most clearly non-existent.
I told the lads we'd bring him home
to you that *very* instant."

"A risky little gamble, but I must
commend your pluck.
It seems we have encountered
a reversal of our luck.

"There's many things that one can do
with prisoners like these.
A ransom comes to mind,
or else a stew that's sure to please."

"You'll not submerge me in a stew,
nor broil me medium-well.
Though void of spells I *still* can throw
a curse, good King Narzell!"

The faery king then gnashed his teeth
(all six he still possessed)
and slammed his cane upon the bier,
then beat his withered breast.

"What jack-o-lantern pixie,
and what foul, putrescent fool,
gave this lout my *name*
that he might use it as a tool?"

The captain of the faeries quailed,
his heart beat like a hammer.
But I piped-up before he had
a chance to even stammer.

"I didn't get your moniker
from any of these slaves.
I heard it whispered on the wind
while passing by some graves.

"Two wraiths upon a headstone
Were discussing gates to Hell.
I heard one say this woodland
was the fief of King Narzell."

The monarch clenched his fist
and then he pounded on his throne.
"Your father is a goat!" he snarled.
"Your mother is a crone!"

A crylvane dropped its spool of thread
and ventured to inquire,
"If he's without his magic,
then why *can't* we eat him, Sire?"

The ruler cast a bloodshot eye
upon his creep-in-waiting.
Without a doubt such ignorance
a royal nerve was grating.

"What bitter gods have scorned me?"
sighed the King in weary woe.
"That I'm surrounded by the sorts
of fiends that do not know …

"…a sorcerer who lacks the strength
to douse a candle-flame
can still employ his dying breath
to curse us all by name!

"And I, for one, have had my fill,"
he added with a growl.
"The last three hundred years have seen
our fortunes turn most foul.

"Thus, no, we cannot feast on him,
not one delicious slice.
But just because we play it safe
does *not* mean we play nice!"

"I fathom your dilemma, King,"
I said, still on the ground.
"We could reach some agreement
were I not completely bound."

"Tied up you shall remain
until I craft a proper jail,
and lest you fancy torture,
you had *best* tell us your tale."

King Narzell then gestured
to the mortal girl I'd seen.
"Miranda, bring those pens of yours,
you worthless human teen!

"I want his tale recorded
just in case we must compose
a ransom-letter to the richest
witches that he knows."

The red-haired waif, Miranda,
in her puffed-out overcoat,
approached the bier with pen and pad.
The King clutched at her throat.

"Changeling, who's your master?
Oh, changeling, who's your king?
Dear changeling, who's the one for whom
you must do *any* thing?"

"It's you," the girl Miranda said,
"Your will and nothing more."
And then she rolled her eyes a bit;
she'd been through this before.

The old one pointed at me, then,
his features most insane.
"Now speak, O warlock, tell us why
you've entered my domain."

"I have no wish to bore you, Sire,
with dreary wizard jargon.
But if I tell the tale in full …
will you concede to bargain?

"The moods of faery folk can be
most treacherous, it's true.
I was a friend of Orpheus.
I *know* what you can do."

"How lovely," King Narzell replied.
"You sense this is no game.
Now launch your tale forthwith
and do begin it with a name!"

Sitting up as best I could,
I watched Miranda raise,
a pen to note the first five words:
"My name is Rowan Blaize.

"I did not mean to trespass and,
as noted to your fey,
I climbed the craggy oak to dodge
the rain that fell today.

"Yet my conundrum started
with *another* pesky storm.
Two days ago I flew up from
Morocco, dry and warm.

"Some friends had gathered west of Fez,
a small reunion, really.
We sat atop the columns of the
ruins at WaLee-Lee.

"We basked and drank ambrosia
and discussed the bygone days
of the city in its glory
and our most amusing stays.

"By afternoon we'd had enough,
the desert wind depressed us.
Lost in our nostalgia,
crumbling temples soon distressed us.

" 'We ought to meet at Philae,' "
said one friend to cheer our hearts.
" 'It's loveliest before the mortal
tourist season starts.'

" 'The temples there are well-preserved,' "
another friend agreed.
" 'If I weren't due in Amsterdam,
I'd fly at lightning speed!'

"Eventually, we learned each one
had someplace else to be.
But little did I know
my destination was a tree!"

"We said farewells and then we all
took off to places varied.
My spells were working soundly,
on the wind most safely carried.

"About an hour later,
as I soared above the sea,
I started feeling rather tired,
A rarity for me.

"I'd planned to stop in London
and the distance wasn't daunting.
Much farther have I travelled
to the spots I'm fond of haunting.

"The weather started grumbling
when I reached the South of France.
A wind-shear sent me spinning
in a most unsightly dance.

"Yet, things like that can happen
to the most innately gifted.
I summoned faithful Zephyr
and above the cloud-bank lifted.

"But as I pierced the icy air
my sense of space felt skewed,
and slowly I began to note
a loss of altitude.

"The clouds below kept getting close
as swifter I was sinking.
A few more spells of fortitude
I muttered, barely thinking.

"The strange malaise seemed conquered
by the time I got to Paris,
but when I reached the Channel
I was once again embarrassed.

"A massive storm was waiting there
to greet me in the dusk.
A looming walrus-of-a-cloud,
with *me* beneath its tusk!

" 'Twas then my powers left me
much like water down a drain.
The grasping maelstrom had me …
I could not withstand the strain.

"The remnants of the spells I cast
were all that kept me going.
Last dregs of dwindling magic
from my desperate soul went flowing.

"I rode the racing storm as best I could
and then was thrown
into a muddy barnyard down the road,
hurled like a stone.

"A kindly mortal farmer took me in
and offered aid.
Yet now from my pursuits
by your dear guard I am waylaid.

"This most unpleasant treatment
is a scandal, at the least.
A mortal grants me refuge,
but *you* treat me like a beast?"

The ancient king threw back his head
and nearly lost his crown.
He chortled loud and long,
as did his subjects all around.

"You ought to thank your lucky stars,"
at last the Old One said.
"If other mortals you had met,
I daresay you'd be dead!

"For humankind *these* days
is hardly known for graciousness.
But then again, that's nothing new.
They're jackals, more or less.

"Yet mortals don't concern me
at the moment, though I could
regale you with the ways in which
they fail to be much good.

"Our interest lies with you,
my sad and luckless little thing,
my sorcerer who claims to be
a bird-with-broken-wing.

"Untimely loss of magic
is a subject I know well.
What caused your grand malfunction, witch?
What nullified your spell?"

"This quandary consumes me
as we speak, O wizened host.
There is no likely theory
of which I might care to boast.

"Had someone placed a spell on me
I would have sensed its hold.
Moreover, no one in my world
would *dare* to be so bold."

"On that count I believe you,"
said the King with fiery gaze.
"For I have heard at whiles
of the amazing Rowan Blaize.

"I never thought I'd meet a mage
of your outstanding stock.
To see one now so helpless
is a most intriguing shock!

"Your mother's escapades around
these isles are quite well-known.
I need not add your father spurred
some legends of his own.

"One wonders what fine price you'd fetch
if either of them knew
their celebrated offspring
had been captured by my crew.

"Perhaps they'd not believe it,
for your *own* great reputation
is admired throughout the lands by
Magic-Folk of every station.

"If you are who you claim to be,
then I am duly thrilled
to have within my clutches one
who dragon-kind has killed!

"Oh yes, the tales have circulated—
word has widely spread
of mighty Rowan Blaize
who fought the Graul and left him dead!

"If memory serves correctly
I can still recall the days
when knights quailed in their armor
at the name of Rowan Blaize.

"Bandits of the Warwing Pass
transformed to silent stone,
and ogres of the Butcher Bogs
reduced to ash and bone.

"In fact your talents rank you,
I've been made to understand,
the glory of your bloodline
and the pride of your whole clan!

"Though down-at-heel ourselves, of late,
there's hope to be restored.
We'll send forth ultimatums
and collect our due reward.

"And lest your parents question me,
or doubt that you are here,
I'll nip denials in the bud
by sending them an ear!

"This is a mere formality,
I'm sure you'll never miss it.
When viewed within a gift box
they'll be hard-pressed to dismiss it.

"So now bring forth a dagger
and make brief our guest's distress.
The only thing we need from him
is Mum and Dad's address."

At this, my turn to laugh arrived.
I bellowed till I ached.
"O King Narzell," I managed,
"you have made a grand mistake!

"For one thing I have not seen 'Mum'
in some few hundred years.
The last I heard she haunts
a mountain range in west Tangiers.

"My father no one's seen since he
encountered Archon Gate.
He entered new dimensions and
we do not know his fate.

"And even if they *were* around
to pester with extortion,
they'd never be impressed
by body parts, whatever portion.

"The members of my clan
aren't very close, to put it mildly.
We're left alone to live our lives
apart, however wildly."

"You obfuscate!" Narzell retorted,
snarling in his rage.
"I've ransomed witches off before.
Don't *try* to trick us, mage!"

"Your sordid past transactions
don't concern me in the least."
I stared the fey-king down as he
was huffing like a beast.

"I can't imagine any witch
who's worthy of their name,
would let you get away with such
a tawdry little game."

"I fear no repercussions," said the King
'neath arching brow.
"We make all parties sign, up-front,
the hallowed Blood-Script Vow."

"It seems you've thought of everything,
but that does not surprise me.
I'm more at loss for reasons why
your court should so despise me."

"As if you'd truly care to know
the problems of my kind."
The King's head bowed in sadness.
Something weighed upon his mind.

"You did not even realize
that we dwell in this wood.
About the globe you flit and fly …
at least till *now* you could.

"We held our own for ages
in this verdant woodland realm.
As man and his machines closed-in,
I faltered at the helm.

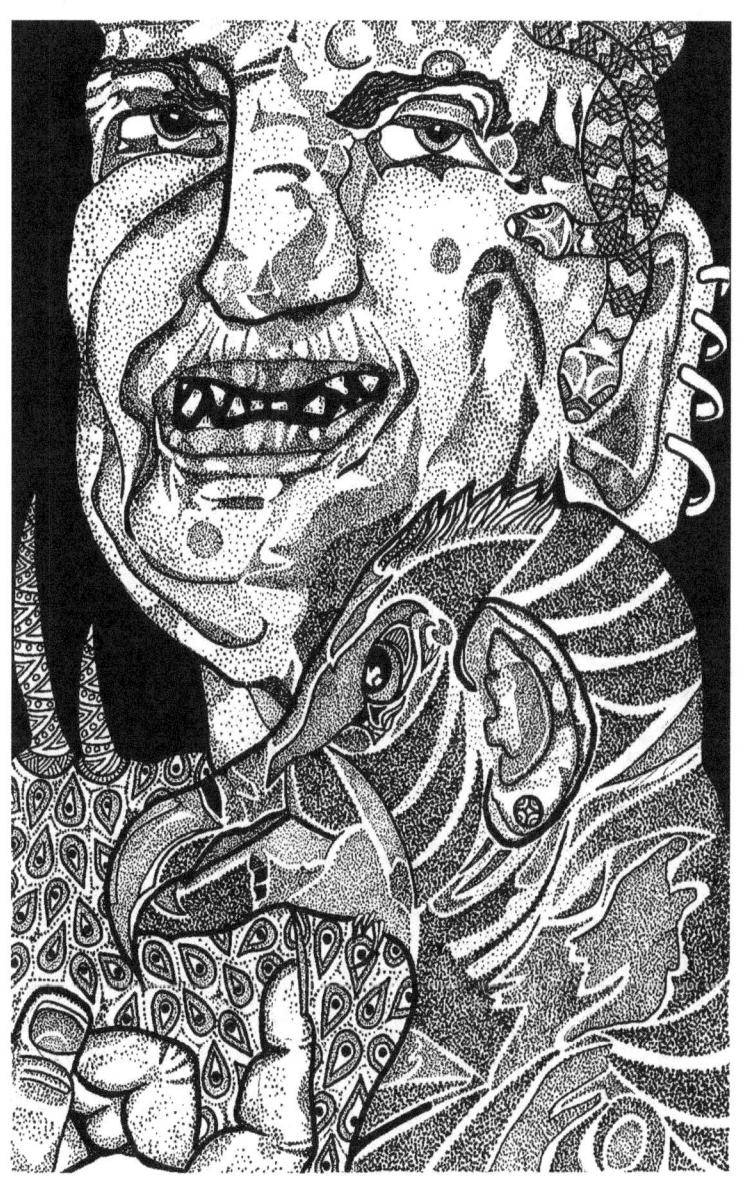

"Reduced each year by callousness,
each falling tree a sign
of our great diminution
in the mortals' foul design.

"Where once the people trembled
in the darkness of their hovels,
they chipped away at *our* domain
with axes and with shovels.

"No more were proper offerings
on doorsteps nightly placed.
No whispered prayers from hunters
who with woodland treks were faced.

"By magic and by mischief
we attempted to prevent
this exile to the margins,
but our foes would *not* relent!

"Where once these forests teemed
with faery life and jubilation,
we find ourselves the members of
a worn and shrunken nation.

"Some say we should be grateful
for what woodland still remains,
for those within the mortal world
who've always taken pains

"… to see that little forests, here and there,
are well-preserved,
that tiny parks and trails
for their amusement are reserved.

"These 'habitats' of which they speak
are stripped of inner-glory.
No longer lives the Magic Wood
of ancient song and story!

"Tis thus you find collected here
the last to guard their home.
The flotsam and the jetsam
of renowned Mad Ramble's Roam.

"Unlike your kind, dear Rowan Blaize,
our sort cannot adapt
or waltz with ease in mortal circles
lest we should be trapped.

"But trapped we are in any case,
for to this paltry wood,
we're bound like twisted tree roots
and in exile here for good.

"The day shall come when mortal folly
fells the final tree,
and when that happens, Rowan Blaize,
our kind shall cease to *be*.

"What time remains, however,
shall be used to weave a plan
and undermine our enemies
in every way we can.

"A trick or two we still possess
up sleeves of many sorts,
for fey and imp and crylvane
make the finest of cohorts!

"And since our lot's been pushed
to this peripheral existence,
all who care to trespass
must remain at my insistence."

Then King Narzell sat rigid
on the cracked and ruined throne.
He gazed across the gathered
for approval from his own.

The crylvanes howled agreement
and the shadwocks all applauded.
The dryads ululated and their King
each goblin lauded.

All members of the faery army
registered their thanks
by hoisting every tiny spear
aloft as one phalanx.

And I, despite captivity,
could not suppress a pang
of sadness at the ragged pride
with which the wood-mob sang.

The only one who failed to cheer
that tattered monarch's speech
was young red-haired Miranda,
her approval out of reach.

She'd spent the whole time scribbling-out
the ruler's long lament,
and now, as pen and paper drooped,
her skills as scribe were spent.

She blew a bubble with her gum
as soon the din died down.
I wondered how the King had come
to keep this child around.

Yet answers on that matter
were most clearly not forthcoming.
The werebeasts moved much closer
and the nixies started humming.

"Behold, our lord has spoken,"
said one spirit in my ear.
"The prisoner may *now* reply
unless he's rapt with fear!"

"The only thing with which I'm 'wrapped'
are these confounded cords.
I'd have more room to breathe
if you would cut them with your swords."

"Release is not an option," said the King,
"and furthermore,
by wily warlocks we've been tricked
too many times before."

"Since I'm no good for ransom
and my flesh you can't consume,
you're wise enough to set me free
at *some* point, I presume?"

"You mustn't cut him loose, my lord,
for there's no guarantee
he won't return and take revenge
on poor folk such as we!"

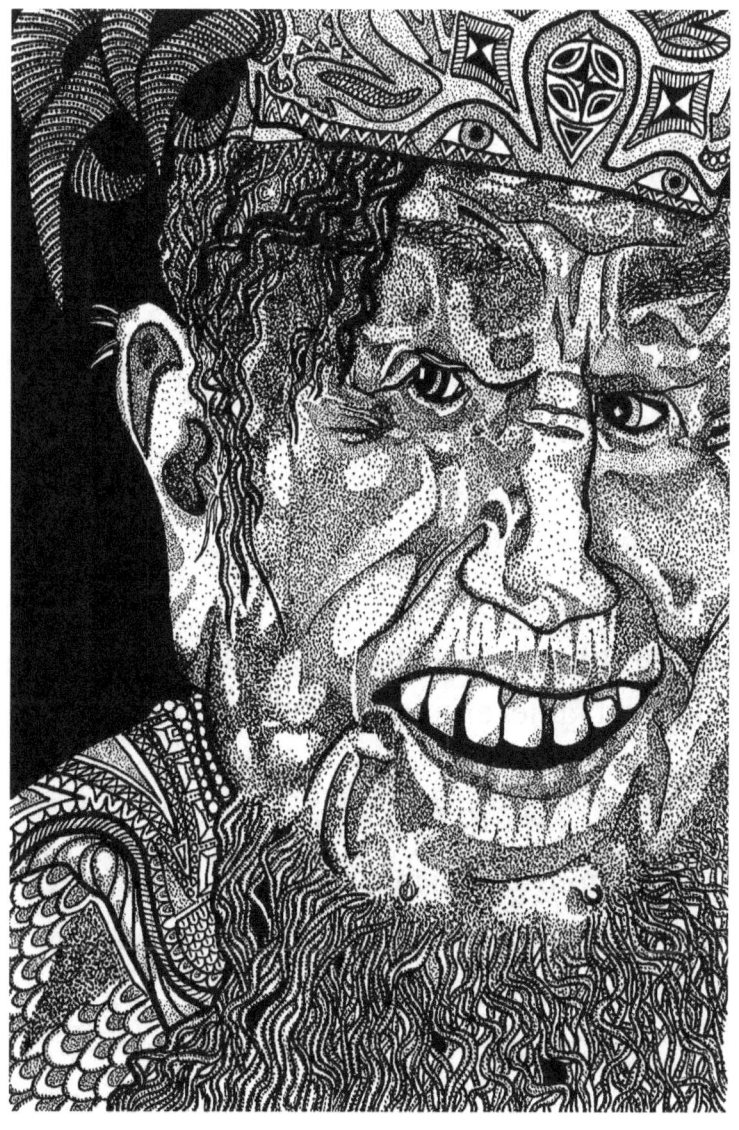

This last a lowly crylvane slobbered
in the royal ear.
Narzell, in anger, shoved him off
as next an imp drew near.

"I feels it in me rotten bones—
you must not heed him, Sire.
Without a doubt he shall return
and scorch us all with fire!"

"Back off, you whining cowards,
I do *not* require advice.
There still may be a way this fool
can fetch a decent price."

"I feel for your decline, Narzell,"
I murmured in the murk.
"But there's no way your plan
to sell-me-on shall ever work.

"Employ the kingly wisdom
which for centuries you've stored.
Release me now and I do vow
to offer grand reward."

The faery ring grew silent,
save for snapping bonfire flame.
Narzell just blinked his bulbous eyes,
with venom spat my name:

"Rowan Blaize, I won't abide
a word you say to me.
Your vow I shan't believe
nor do I fear your sorcery!"

"And as for kingly wisdom
I shall put it to the test.
Now off you go until I hatch
a plot I think is best!"

With that, he raised his gnarled cane
and spoke a faery spell.
Then upward I was lifted
to be hurled across the dell.

VI

THE CHANGELING OF THE EMERALD BLADE

One quail in fowler's net ensnared,
all power to resist impaired;
the plaything of misfortune's whim
upon a night most damp and grim.
My London goal, alas, no nearer …
gruesome fate, however, clearer.
Morning blackness lingered on.
What *new* defeat would come with dawn?

The cane of King Narzell had proved
his powers weren't as spent
as one might otherwise deduce
from one so old and bent.

Nor were his claims of faded strength
so blatantly transparent;
the old toad still had gumption
and that much was now apparent.

In deeper woods I had been flung
and then I had been thrown
into a net of banshee hair
the crylvane brood had sewn.

How wise that King Narzell a net
of *this* kind had provisioned,
since banshee locks possess the power
to keep a mage imprisoned.

While cramped into a painful ball
and slung across a bough
the faery noise subsided—only
wind could I hear now.

It whistled and it hooted
like some owl with iron lungs,
and through the treetops rustled leaves
that clucked and flapped like tongues.

Where the King and court had gone
could not at all be seen.
They vanished from that lonesome place
as if they'd never been.

So there I swung most gently
as the banshee netting creaked,
when suddenly from 'round
an aging alder someone peeked.

"How now?" I croaked as best I could,
my throat completely crunched,
and tried to move my hands which were
around my ankles bunched.

"It's only me, Miranda,"
said a whisper on the breeze.
She walked into a moonlight beam
that strayed among the trees.

On tip-toe she approached me
and then stared with tilted head.
"You sorcerers are tough …
I half-expected you'd be dead."

"Clearly, mortal child, about my kind
you're misinformed.
I've bested greater foes
and I have weathered fiercer storms."

"No need for you to talk to me
as if I was a kid.
I turned fourteen last year, you know.
At least I *think* I did."

Her soft green eyes reflected
starlight glimmer where she stood.
I felt like any monkey in some
caged exhibit would.

"I'm sure your vaunted master
would stir-up a hornet's nest
if he *knew* that you were here …
or are you here at his behest?"

Miranda merely shook her head
and shrugged her shoulders once.
"Narzell's asleep and I'm not scared
to pull these kinds of stunts."

"I learned to throw the dryads
off my trail," she said with pride.
"And from those nosy crylvanes
it's no sweat to run and hide.

"The King's still pretty wary
but his head is getting odd.
He'd bash me if he knew
the many roads that I have trod.

"His crabby little army treats me
like some stupid punk.
But I can lose them when I wish,
'cos half the time they're drunk.

"The rest are either fading fast
or too afraid to tell
if ever they should see me
wander off from Ramble's Dell.

"The wicked part of this
is that they need me to survive.
I'm sent to town to steal the stuff
that keeps them all alive."

"What's this?" I gasped in wonderment.
"You walk amongst your kind?
I'd think first chance you'd run away
and leave these freaks behind!"

"I fear it's not that easy,"
said Miranda, sighing low.
"For one, there is the spell, and
then I've got no place to go.

"See, long ago the King sent out
his finest shadwock scout,
who found me in my crib
and with a piglet switched me out.

"And ever since, they raised me here,
in this ungodly place.
A spell was put upon me
so I'd not forsake home-base.

"Whenever I got old enough
to run the errands needed,
they sent me to the towns but saw
that all commands were heeded.

"The magic made it easy
to explore most anywhere.
People looked right at me as I stole,
but didn't care.

"They'd nod their heads and smile
like I was just some harmless waif.
I'd fill my bag with crazy loot
and back I'd come, quite safe.

"Sometimes I do *my* thing in town
and linger half the day,
just watching all the faces
of the folk who pass my way.

"Years ago, I overheard
some biddy in a wig
discuss two tragic people
who were raising-up a pig!

"She said no one in town
believed the story going 'round
of how this couple's babe was taken
… and the oinker found.

"Apparently police had launched
some big investigation.
The couple disappeared.
It was believed they fled the nation.

"A most pathetic tale,"
I gurgled sadly in the net.
"But faeries in the best of times
have craved a human pet."

"This life is all I've ever known,"
Miranda said, unmoved.
"And even if I tried to tell
it never could be proved.

"It's not all bad, there are a few
concessions, heaven knows.
They let me steal the books I like
and wear these mortal clothes.

"For them I bring back jewelry,
or bags of safety pins.
I lug big jars of marmalade and
junk from garbage bins.

"But, best of all, the King allows me
lots of drawing paper,
and I can swipe a brand new set
of pens with every caper.

"The one thing that I wanted to bring back
and keep myself
was just a sad-eyed puppy
lounging on a pet shop shelf.

I promised I would care for it
and never ask for help.
The King then boxed my ears
and said, 'Forget about that whelp!'

"It was a disappointment
and, of that, there's no mistake.
Since then I've learned to be content
with other stuff I take.

"When I first started venturing
to town for our supplies,
I'd hang out in the bookstores
and on art would feast my eyes.

"Abstracts, comics, classics—
I loved everything I saw,
and pretty soon I taught myself
to read and write and draw.

"Now drawing is the thing I love
the most in all the world."
She reached into a pocket
and produced a paper curled.

"The King says it's a waste of time.
The hags and nixies snort.
The shadwocks can't be bothered,
so they tear it up, for sport.

"Still, maybe *you* could have a look;
you've been so many places.
The King thinks it's a joke,
But ... do you think I'm good at faces?"

Miranda held the drawing up
and in the meager light,
I glimpsed the fourteen years of loss,
of loneliness and fright.

"Mortal child, I say this now
and all these words are true:
If ever I compose my tale
the drawings *you* must do."

"That's nice of you to say,
as no one hardly seems to care.
The best I've ever gotten is an
unbelieving stare."

"That is a shame and doubt me not,
but worse, of course, the pity
that I shall never write *my* tale
or make it to the city."

"You mustn't give up every hope,"
Miranda then instructed.
"I came 'cos we have much in common,
both of us abducted.

"This banshee net's the strongest
one I've seen in all my life.
But Screamers' hair don't stand a chance
against an emerald knife.

"I grabbed this from the King's own trove
and not a peep I made."
From deep inside her pocket
came a green and glowing blade.

VII

OF BLOODWORM PIPES AND TELLTALE IMPS

London dripped with cold regard
from Tunbridge Wells to Scotland Yard.
Resentment festered, block by block,
empowered by the ancient rock
and coddled by a rolling mist
that loveless ocean water kissed.
Yet, London's ardor summoned me …
alone, unmatched in majesty.

Praised indeed be London's dinge,
its clammy, brief embrace.
When darkness oozed through cobbled streets
I found my Auntie's place.

Since liberation from the net
Of King Narzell's designs,
I'd brushed aside the forest trap
and clutching faery vines.

From dawn till Auntie's doorstep,
marching onward to the city,
I stopped for neither rest nor ride,
eschewing all self-pity.

Though even worse-for-wear I looked
than after Sunday's storm,
among the streetwise mortal youth
my garb appeared the norm.

In *this* way I was most equipped
to travel free from harm.
At other times such camouflage
requires a potent charm.

My dear Aunt Ariadne owns
a home in Holland Park.
Its grandeur much like others
clustered 'round it in the dark.

This stone four-storied structure
(built when Edward ruled the land)
is one of nine or ten that "Auntie Addie"
keeps on hand.

Unlike my other relatives,
old Addy loves to mingle
with mortal high society
and furthermore she's single.

For these two reasons and a few
I would not care to mention,
her status in our family
is fraught with nervous tension.

Although she's called "eccentric"
no one says so to her face.
You'd *never* want my Aunt
to have to put you in your place.

I staggered up the marble steps
and lingered on the bell.
At other times I've entered
through the chimney, via spell!

I thought not for a moment
that my Aunt would get the door,
but still I was dismayed to see
her trusty servant, Bror.

He's been with her for centuries,
I cannot fathom why.
I'd never keep a servant
of such condescending eye.

And when I speak of "eye"
I mean exactly what I say.
He has the right but how he lost
the left … no one will say.

So there he was before me,
peering out into the fog.
My Auntie's eight-foot henchman,
her devoted servant-dog.

And when I speak of dog
I am not meaning to insult,
For Bror was once a Mastiff
and *this* form is the result

of one of Auntie Addie's most
select and special spells.
She likes Bror better as a man
without the Mastiff smells.

Yet never have I cared for Bror
and daresay that he knows it.
Deep down I hate his arrogance
and frequently he shows it.

When one has been for centuries
A witch's dog-made-man,
I guess one feels entitled
to be haughty when one can.

But never in the years that I
have known this towering tree
did he possess more reason
to look down his snout at me.

"I do declare!" dull Bror intoned
and looked me up and down.
"You must be something Leto's cat
dragged screaming into town."

His voice a distant foghorn booming
from the edge of Hell,
he lowed as would a turgid moose
that wasn't feeling well.

"I have no use for snide remarks
and less for dirty looks.
So let me in, old chap,
I need to scour my Auntie's books."

"You're in a fix, it's plain to see,"
said Bror and how he drooled!
His spit dripped down from Mastiff fangs
and at my feet it pooled.

"One finds it rather shocking
To behold your sad condition.
But enter freely, Most Unkempt,
You don't need *my* permission."

"That's right, my friend, so move aside.
Do not deter my way.
I'd love to stay and chat
but it has been a trying day."

Nudging past the hulking oaf,
I stepped into the hall,
The heel of one worn boot gave way
and spun me toward the wall.

"It's worse than I suspected,
your arrival at this hour.
Unless I'm much mistaken,
it would seem you've lost your power!"

Grappling with the statue
of a centaur near the door,
I stoop up on my tip-toes
with a finger fixed on Bror.

"Now hear me well, I'll take no cheek
from *you,* ungainly brute.
You're nothing but a canine
in a magic human-suit.

"The nonsense I've endured
the past few days is not some joke.
On humble pie aplenty
I've been forced to nearly choke.

"Instead of standing 'round
like some malignant, gloating troll,
you *might* find ways to help me
claw my way up from this hole.

"Remember, by your mistress
I am favored most of all
among our noble family
and its members great and small.

"Remember, too, that even though
my strength is compromised,
my power rivals Auntie's
and is *not* to be despised.

"So do yourself a service
and be swift to heed my plea.
I've come to see old Addy—
Kindly say where she might be!"

By then Bror's lips were trembling
and each hand hid in a pocket.
The patch upon his missing eye
had slipped below the socket.

He bowed his head and drooled a bit
for I was on the edge.
He knew that I would drag him down
if pushed off from the ledge.

"My tongue *does* get the best of me,"
he stammered to explain.
"Please disregard my insolence,
ignore my fevered brain!

"The gall that I display
is most unfit in the extreme.
Yet know my tart rejoinders
are not always what they seem.

"If I, perchance, were happy,
as I was in ancient days …
you would not have to suffer
my uncouth, resentful ways."

Bror's bizarre apology
was tense and enigmatic.
Though tempted to hear every bit,
my goals remained pragmatic.

"Without a doubt your tale is sad
and laden well with grief.
But do as I commanded, Bror,
and make your answer brief!"

"Your aunt is in her study,"
he replied through bubbling spit.
"I brought her tea an hour ago
and then her pipe I lit."

"Then off you go to see about
the evening's other cares.
Don't *dare* to even follow—
I can show myself upstairs."

With that the gloomy butler
bowed into a nearby hall.
His figure stooped for, in that
passageway, he was too tall.

Then through the musty house
I stomped right up its winding flights,
and as I went I savored all the
grand, familiar sights.

My dear old Auntie Addy keeps
each home that she has built
well-stocked with gathered spoil
and decorated to the hilt.

The walls are jammed with portraits
of the famous and obscure.
Each niche is filled with work by sculptors
Addy deigned to lure.

All through her long, eventful life
my Aunt ensnared the hearts
of many massive talents
as a "Patron of the Arts."

Indeed, a few practitioners
who'd crossed her in some fashion,
were here and there preserved in stone,
their faces cool and ashen.

A harpist on the second floor,
some actor on the third.
The drone of Addy's spell
the final sound they'd ever heard.

My Aunt was not inclined to such abuse
—at least not often—
And, over time, her most ill-tempered
moods began to soften.

Yet, in her day she was
a fabled beauty and, with that,
there comes a tendency to play
the role of "spoiled brat."

When childishness is coupled
with a witch's awful strength,
the cavalier who draw too near
will meet their doom, at length.

But long ago have passed the days
since Addy prowled about
for handsome mortal men to entertain
… and then throw out.

Still, those unlucky few she "kept"
now stand in grim reminder
that when a witch is kind to you
it's best to treat her *kinder*.

Few well-heeled men solicit
Auntie's favor anymore,
and woe to any robber who
attempts to breach her door.

For while the local gentry
need alarms to guard their wealth,
and bars are placed on windows
to preserve domestic health …

… my old Aunt Ariadne
has no need for such effects.
Her power any interloper
crushes or deflects.

Once, a masked intruder snuck-in,
quiet as a mouse,
and to his great misfortune
found a demon "keeping house."

When witches go on holiday
they never need to worry.
Nor would you if *you* could conjure
werewolves fanged and furry.

At last, up to the study doors
I crept, my body reeling,
The candlelight around
cast dancing shadows on the ceiling.

I flung the doors wide open
and was most relieved to see
my old, decrepit Auntie
slurping at her cup of tea.

This was Ariadne,
once a vixen world-renowned.
A grizzled Dame with thinning hair,
her body squat and round.

She wore her blackest knee-length dress
and in a chair was rocking.
I noticed as I entered quite a run
upside her stocking.

She glanced up from the book
that she was reading and she squinted.
Upon her black and beady eyes
the light of hearthside glinted.

The teacup rattled on the saucer
as she set it down.
The smile between her wrinkled apple
cheeks became a frown.

Taking one great puff upon
the pipe that she was smoking,
she next began to cackle
as if someone near were joking.

"By the craggy shores of Naxos
and the Knot of mighty Isis,
it seems beloved Rowan's come
to Auntie in some crisis!

"It looks like Hades' hound
has chewed you up and spit you out.
Come in, bedraggled dear, and tell me:
What's this all about?"

"I must confess, Aunt Addy,
it's a joy to hear your voice.
To bother you revolts me
but I have no other choice."

"Oh, stop with all that nonsense,"
she replied and gave a wink.
"Sit down beside your favorite aunt
and have a little drink."

Her gnarled hand reached out
and with a croaking, mumbled spell,
she filled an empty glass nearby
with wine … and filled it well!

I took it from the table
and slumped down into a chair.
The sweet scent of ambrosia filled
the study's stifling air.

In one long gulp the glass was empty;
Auntie's eyes grew wide.
I put my head back on the seat
and with delight I sighed.

"Not bad, that little potion,"
Auntie said and puffed away.
"A trick that Dionysus taught me
way back in the day."

"It's positively radiant,"
I managed then to mumble.
"At this point if you fed me tar
I'd scarcely even grumble."

"Oh ho, my boy, that's quite a statement.
Certainly you jest.
But I can see that something's
put you sorely to the test.

"Don't tell me you've been fighting
with your mother once again.
I've warned you to avoid her
since I can't remember when.

"That woman hasn't been the same
since Enoch left her side.
He only crossed to Abarat—
it's not as if he died!"

"With Mother I have not been tangling,
nor have I contended
with dragons of the Halpern Caves.
Those fences *have* been mended.

"This problem is more worrisome
than anything I've faced,
for all my power left me
and my magic's been displaced!"

"Now that's another matter,"
muttered Auntie in surprise.
"A thing like that will always cut
the strongest down to size.

"And you, my lad, have always
shown us brilliant work to spare.
To see you here in such a state
is quite beyond compare.

"A total loss of sorcery
I never would have guessed.
But now you've come to me
and we can ponder what is best."

"How strange," I said, "your servant Bror
knew well my awful plight.
And he is not the only one
who guessed this illness right."

"Ha!" Aunt Addy bellowed
as the smoke curled 'round her head.
"A non-witch is the *first* to guess
the thing all witches dread.

"You see, they're ever-hopeful
that, at any given hour,
they'll stumble on a witch or warlock
robbed of all their power.

"It's been the same old story
since the Ruling Ones came down,
and long before the first cave-dwelling
mortals were around.

"When demi-gods are weakened,
that's the time they make their move.
It's always been a power-struggle
rife with things to prove.

"Bror is quite like all the rest
who to this earth are bound
But what can you expect from him?
He's really just a hound!"

"Yet still your faithful servant,"
I replied, "although he's bitter.
Perhaps you should have chosen one
from some more noble litter."

Auntie Addy waved a hand,
dismissing my concern
"Bror can be a trial, at times,
but *I* forced him to learn.

"This is what our kind must do
For we know what is best.
So long as balance *is* maintained,
who cares about the rest?"

With this, she held a crooked finger
toward my slumping form
and in my brain came rushing back
the horror of the storm.

The whole effect was shocking, almost like
I'd been attacked.
My Auntie twitched her finger once
and then she drew it back.

"Ye gods, what sort of vile and painful probe
was *that?*" I gasped.
"The source of your complaint," she answered,
"*must* be firmly grasped.

"Alas, the only thing I saw
was you, caught in a gale.
I sense no spell upon you,
so you'd best recount your tale.

She filled her pipe with something
squirming in an ivory box,
and sat back in her chair to watch
and listen like a fox.

I told her of the luncheon
with my friends in old WaLeeLee.
She grunted once and puffed some more,
her gaze most sharp and steely.

The drama of the tempest
was recounted for her pleasure,
as was my night with Farmer Mould,
his kindness beyond measure.

Two brows rose up with interest
when I told her of Narzell,
and of his faery gypsy-camp
that languished in the dell.

"I knew him long ago, my boy,
when London still was young.
Of his once-lavish court
were many songs composed and sung.

"But he was one of several faery kings
throughout the lands.
So many of them vanished
at the wrath of mortal hands.

"One has to give him credit
for surviving there at *all*.
It's lucky you escaped and that
Fortuna heard your call."

"That's well and good, my dearest Aunt,
but still the riddle beckons.
Why did my powers fail me
in a matter of mere seconds?"

Auntie Ariadne breathed
a sigh toward the fire.
The waning flame within the hearth
roared merrily and higher.

The corners of the study
soon with living shadows filled.
They whispered by the cases crammed
with ancient books and spilled

along the woodwork carved
with scenes of wild, forbidden rites,
and with these revels merged
to form intoxicating sights.

The chamber seemed to tremble
with enchantment that delivered
some fleeting sense of hope and,
as it fled, my Auntie shivered.

"Rowan, this calamity,
must be resolved with skill.
But I cannot restore your magic
swiftly or at will.

"At first, I thought some curse
among those ruins was to blame.
For places of that sort have long
deserved their wicked fame …

"… as scenes where spells primeval
and lamenting spirits linger,
waiting for someone at whom
to point a wretched finger.

"Waleelee, of all places,
is a haunt of banished djinn,
who in their lonely exile seek
to multiply their sin.

"The most accomplished sorcerer
can soon become their prey
if traipsing there unwary
by the night or in the day.

"Yet you, dear lad, are far too wise
for some cast-off Afreet,
and equally too grand to be
brought down by hail and sleet.

"The storm did not reduce you
and the ruins did no harm.
Nor do you seem bedeviled
by some other mage's charm.

"There *is* one way, however,
your travail I may discern.
Let's conjure-up a GnostiKimp
and see what we can learn!"

"A GnostiKimp, you say, my Auntie?
What a stroke of brilliance!
Though summoning a thing like that
requires a keen resilience.

"I haven't summoned one of those
since Father first departed.
The sentient little beast held back
and left us broken hearted.

"But Auntie, if you think it best
I'd like the problem solved.
You're sure that you recall the spell?
It's rather quite involved."

"What? You doubting youngster!
Do you think that I've gone daft?
Do all these silly wrinkles mean
I can't maintain my craft?

"I've been around six thousand years
in this world and in others,
not always as you see me now
and *if* I had my druthers …

"… the looks I owned when youthful
would stay with me 'round the clock.
But spells *that* vain invite one's peers
to mutter and to mock.

"The mortals grow old gracefully,
at least by surgeon's hand.
Would serve them best to honor Time's
unending pour of sand.

"Besides, when so desired,
I'm still as lovely as the rest.
Make no mistake, your Aunt can cast
a glamour with the best!"

To prove the point she passed a claw
along her flabby frame.
Within an instant, there she was—
The Ivory Maid of fame.

"Behold, I haven't lost my touch,"
she growled with a frown.
"And in this scintillating form
I'll bind a demon *down!*"

The ancient Persian carpet
in the study was thrown back.
Beneath it was a pentagram
with sigils carved in black.

She raised her now translucent arms
and mesmerized the air.
Behind the fire roared applause
as I cringed in my chair.

I watched in fascination—
this was going to be a show.
What caliber of imp she'd call
I truly did not know.

"Denizens of Hidden Spheres!
O Eyes Behind the Veil!
Unfettered Sibyl spirits who
upon the swift wind sail!
Ye foul and reckless demons
of the festering Abyss,
Now hearken to this mighty spell
and don't ye dare resist!
From all forgotten corners
of the worlds and Worlds-Within,
from every secret landscape
let relentless search begin.
For I, great Ariadne, seek an imp
to do my will.
A seer among demon-kind,
one willing to fulfill
the task I have appointed
so that Truth be duly found.
Arise, O GnostiKimp,
within this pentagram be BOUND!"

An incandescent burst of light
illumined Auntie's study,
and there, within the circle,
sat a demon rank and ruddy.

It stared at us with bulging orbs
between two crimson horns.
The thing looked like it crawled to us
through centuries of thorns.

Reeking of putrescence,
scabby flesh with blood was oozing.
"To you I come," it groaned.
"But this is *not* of my own choosing."

"If I had known you'd stink like this,"
my Auntie Addy cried,
"I'd summon imps that do not smell
as though their innards died!"

"You weren't expecting roses,"
croaked the devil on the floor.
"It's funny, but no other witch
has dared complain before."

"Well, I am not 'no other witch,'
my whining little slave.
You're here at my disposal,
by the order that I gave."

The creature shrugged a little
as it picked its skanky skin.
"Then, by all means, M'lady,
tell us how we might begin."

"My nephew, here, is stricken
with some ill I can't determine.
Reveal to me its origin at once,
infernal vermin!"

"Auntie, are you certain
that's the way to start things off?
We want *cooperation,* though
I do not mean to scoff."

"Hush now, Rowan,
I know what I'm doing, by and large.
With imps like this it's key
to let them know just *who's* in charge."

"You witches can be tiresome,"
the demon interrupted.
"With grand, inflated egos
you have ever been corrupted."

Ariadne grabbed a poker
from the fireplace
and swung it wide with menace
right before the devil's face.

"I did not ask for commentary,
nor for your opinion.
While trapped within that circle, imp,
I own you as a minion.

"So if you dare ignore
the magic words that I have said,
I'll soon refresh your memory
with iron to the head!"

"It's just a silly poker
that you snatched from over there.
You really think that household tools
can give me such a scare?"

Auntie's eyes turned red with umbrage.
Smoke came out her ears.
She treated her opponent
To the nastiest of sneers.

"Iron, poker, shovel, spoon,
or even sweeping broom.
A household item in *my* hands
Becomes your club of doom!"

"Alright, I get your point.
We must not waste each other's time.
Your nephew is the victim
of a most unpleasant crime.

"He has not been cast down
by evil cause or edict holy.
Four days ago he ate a salad
laced with leaves of moly."

"What?" I screamed and flew up from
the chair in utter shock.
"Ye gods!" exclaimed Aunt Addy
and she hit the floor like rock.

I scampered to her side
but as she pulled away in fear,
she said, "My boy, if moly is involved
please *don't* come near!"

"Auntie, do control yourself
and don't be so outrageous.
If moly is the culprit, then you *know*
I'm not contagious."

"Oh, right you are, my boy,"
she babbled, changing slowly back
into the rotund dowager
enveloped all in black.

"Please pardon my reaction
to this most horrific news.
No wonder we were flummoxed—
moly *never* offers clues!"

"And yet," I asked the GnostiKimp,
still hunched and lurking near,
"How did I miss the presence
of this herb all witches fear?"

"The chef at that small bistro
where you stopped to have your lunch,
mistook a crate of moly
for some basil-by-the-bunch.

"They look and taste the same,
and do forgive if this sounds rude,
but is this *not* one reason
your kind frown on mortal food?"

"I should have been more careful.
Yes, that much is plain to see.
Now speak, all-knowing fellow,
of a cure to offer me!"

The hellspawn made a gruesome face
and shook its bristled brow.
"There *is* no cure for moly.
One should think you'd know by now.

"Besides, I told you all that dwells
within my power to say
Would someone kindly chant the spell
that makes me go away?"

I jiggled Auntie's shoulder;
she was still about to swoon.
In moments she'd be useless
if I didn't rouse her soon.

"It wants to go away," I said.
"Can you produce the spell?
It has no more to offer us,
so send it back to hell."

Out of breath my Auntie dragged
herself up from the floor.
She waved a chubby arm and said,
"Get lost … and stay no more."

"What kind of spell is *that*?"
the imp exclaimed, a bit aghast.
"The least that I deserve
is some short ode or lightning blast."

But Auntie grabbed the poker
she had brandished once before,
and with a grunt of effort
hurled it spinning 'cross the floor.

The GnostiKimp exploded
in a chunky, liquid spray.
The study with its guts was plastered,
dripping mucus gray.

Auntie wheezed and tried to brush
some innards off her sleeve.
"The next time one of *those* comes 'round
he'd best know when to leave!"

"After this I doubt
that any more will care to visit.
Congratulations, Auntie, on a mess
that's most exquisite."

"This is nothing when compared
to some of my old tricks.
Ugh! That demon's brains are sizzling
on the hearthside bricks!"

I threw myself upon the chair,
now thick with devil-slime.
If grimmer news I've ever heard,
I can't recall the time.

Of all the things that can befall
a warlock in his life,
a poisoning by moly
is unrivalled in its strife.

"How stupid that I even asked
the imp about a cure.
A cure does not exist and that's
one thing we know for sure.

"To think that I'm forever doomed
to some earthbound existence!
I'll never fly again with sunrise
looming in the distance.

"My days of changing form
to enter secret worlds are finished.
To endless hours of mortal drudgery
I am diminished.

"Oh Auntie, take the iron rod
you used to club that beast
and do the same to me
or in the very, very least …

"… transform me into something
dull and handy, like a chair.
I'm good for nothing now,
except to hold some derriere!"

Aunt Addy waddled over
and she smoothed my matted mane.
"You must not lose your wits," she said.
"You'll drive yourself insane."

"But *you* know I am finished.
What's left now to discuss?
Moly is a fate that's worse than death
for folk like us."

Auntie took her pipe, still stuffed
with wriggling Bloodworm Weed.
She lit it with a simple word—
I envied her indeed.

"My boy, the outlook isn't grand,
and that I can't deny.
But hope's not lost completely.
There is *one* thing you can try."

"Oh, Auntie, this is *not* the time
for joke or platitude.
Your well-intentioned pity
would do nothing for my mood."

"From me you'll get no pity, Lad,
that's not my cup of tea.
But I might have solutions,
if you'd care to humor me."

"What, you've got a spell that will
undo the herb that smote?
Some potion in your repertoire?
A moly antidote?

Auntie shook her head
and stuck the pipe back in her maw.
"There's nothing in the vast reserve
of spells on which *I* draw.

"Yet, while I may not have the strength
to help you in your plight,
that doesn't mean there isn't
someone *else* I know who might."

"That fried demonic oracle
was rather crystal clear,
and we both know that moly
can't be countered, Auntie dear."

"Rowan, you have always made
this clan extremely proud.
And for your age you've shown
more skill than ought to be allowed.

"But I have more experience
by some four thousand years.
So listen as I seek to soothe
a handful of your fears.

"Throughout the history of our kind
That herb has been a bane,
no matter where it grows,
in each dimension—every plane.

"Not sure I ever mentioned it before,
but you should know,
that when I was a girl
most every summer I would go …

"… to visit this old island
in the blue Aegean Sea.
The sorceress who lived there
was hospitable to me.

"She taught me lots of lovely tricks.
For months on end I stayed.
And for my 'room and board'
I served her gladly as handmaid.

"Mind you, I was not the only
maiden on the isle.
We'd come in droves to serve
the Mistress, lined up rank and file.

"My, but those were lovely times,
when sailors crashed ashore!
We'd lure them in and turn them
into piglets by the score."

"Auntie, don't deceive me.
Were you really there with HER?
No one in magic history
has caused a bigger stir!"

"Oh yes, my dear, I lived there
long ago, each word is true.
Ask your mother—she went out
one summer with me, too."

"I guess I'm just surprised
that no one mentioned this connection.
Yet how does this affect the course
of *my* downward direction?"

"Come now, Rowan,
certainly you know the story well.
How Odie used the moly herb
to break Her greatest spell?

"Believe me when I tell you,
she was *not* a happy lady.
She lost her powers, just like you.
For years her life was shady.

"But, Auntie, many legends claim
she never did recover,
and lived-out all her days
as Odie's angry, jilted lover."

"Don't believe such tales, for most
were told with heaps of spite.
She came back with a vengeance, Luvvy.
Homer got it right."

"You're telling me she found a way
To neutralize the herb?
That all its magic toxin
she was strong enough to curb?"

"She did indeed, my boy,
Though no one knows quite why or how.
She never says a word about those days,
not even now."

"You mean she's still around?
I can't imagine that is true!
Why *she's* four times as old as me,
and twice as old as you."

"Older still than *that,* you pert young thing!
I might have known.
Compared to me, I guess you think
she's four times worse a crone?"

"Of course, I mean no disrespect.
This news I'm still digesting.
And furthermore I'd like to know
just *what* you are suggesting."

"Rowan, I suggest that you
go see her in a hurry.
As luck would have it, last I heard,
she runs a zoo in Surrey!"

"You mean that she is living
only miles away from here?
How could one so famous be
so secret yet so near?"

"She only ever told but two
or three of us, you know.
Her privacy means everything.
She keeps her profile low."

"And I'm supposed to walk right up
and ask her for some help?
She's bound to think me mad,
a most annoying little whelp."

"You've got no choice, poor soul,"
my Auntie sighed, "and even better …
I'll send an introduction
on ahead by formal letter!

"If anyone can tell you how
to beat the Awful Plant,
it's her and no one else.
'Twill be a pity if she can't.

"But first I must call Bror
so he can clean this putrid mess.
And then he'll fetch some clothes,
you can't go out the way you're dressed.

"He'll drive you down tomorrow
Ere the light of dawn has shone.
I don't know what she's like these days,
You *will* be on your own.

"I'm sorry, darling Rowan,
but for *this* odd brand of mercy,
you're going to have to take
the matter up with mighty Circe."

VIII

COLLECTOR'S ITEMS

Fire, river, wind and rock,
Gods among us seldom walk
Instead they burn, they flow, they blow …
through *being* mock what dwells below.
They need no worship to survive
for not one god has been "alive."
Yet when themselves they manifest,
All put the living to the test.

Blinded by a sun that streaked
in ribbons through the air,
I smoothed my velvet sleeves and tweaked
an errant wave of hair

Bror had pulled the limo
with perfection to the curb.
"So *this* is where one goes
to find redemption from the herb?"

I gazed outside the window
at the gate and sign atop.
It read: The Surrey Wildlife Sanctuary
(and Gift Shoppe)

"Madam sent the letter,"
grumbled Bror behind the wheel.
"I watched her wax the envelope
with her own magic seal.

"Then she got the gargoyle
that's been living in the cellar
to fly it out ... but *he* did not return.
I didn't tell her."

"You're quite the little helper, Bror.
You rarely miss a trick.
It's nice to know that you
and Auntie Addy are so thick.

"She told me hardly anything
of Circe's odd endeavor
and swore that she knew nothing,
but I think she's being clever.

"Something strange seems hidden
in the things she *didn't* say.
She was so very adamant
to send me out this way.

"Circe, for her part,
has ever been a grand enigma.
To her attached a most insane,
extraordinary stigma.

"One wonders, loyal Bror,
if there is more you can reveal.
Some added note you managed—just
in passing, mind—to steal?"

"Though I made clear my sadness
as a servant unrewarded,
this life I've lived five hundred years
could never be afforded …

"… without your Aunt's great power
or her strange-but-steadfast ways.
At least with food and shelter
I shall live out all my days.

"Though life may be so thankless
and I dream of youth now lost,
I'd not betray my mistress, Blaize,
for any cause or cost.

"Besides, you need not fear that I
have heard some secret plan.
What she may hatch with peers
does not concern her servant-man.

"For your untimely crisis
I can offer sympathy,
and point the way to Circe's door …
She waits within for thee."

"Then back you go to Auntie, Bror,
I'll pester you no longer.
If we should meet again
I trust you'll find my magic stronger."

To this the ever-drooling Bror
did not deign to reply.
He glanced at me with helplessness
From one great bloodshot eye.

I stepped out from the car
that soon drove off into the day.
The time had come to figure out
what might be best to say.

Concerning someone of the fame
and mystery of Circe,
I was not shocked to hear my Aunt
employ a word like "mercy."

What manner of ambition
may have brought her to this place
was less of a conundrum than
the means of saving face.

Enchantresses of her repute
are seldom void of danger,
and not inclined to trifle
with a power-challenged stranger.

Yet Auntie sent a letter
and she dressed me for the meeting.
The streets around were empty, now;
I pondered proper greeting.

A laughing little mob of mortals
burst out from the doors.
Some children in the group unleashed
a string of beastly roars.

"I liked the lions best," said one.
"The monkeys!" said another.
"Now quiet all, we're heading home
for naps!" exclaimed the mother.

They vanished down the lonesome lane
in something of a hurry.
The spot was on the outskirts
of a woodland park in Surrey.

Emerging from the doorway
in the wake of their departure,
a woman stood beneath the sign
as rigid as an archer.

Her hair was black as pitch
and tied most neatly in a tail
that straight and smooth fell to her waist,
a shining onyx trail.

Upon her young and well-scrubbed face
she wore a pair of glasses.
Behind, her eyelids blinked at me
in lush and languid passes.

Clad in white technician's coat
that draped her wispy frame,
she nodded once and parted lips
as if to call my name.

"They're rather quite annoying
and rambunctious little things."
Her words were tinged with ice
but flew on gentle, satin wings.

"Of what might you be speaking, Miss?"
I asked as she came near.
Her eyes, like blue Aegean seas,
were liquid, harsh, and clear.

She smiled and in the morning chill
her tan complexion blushed.
She studied me from head to toe;
the world, in waiting, hushed.

"Those mortal brats," she murmured,
and then gestured with her chin.
"The kids that just went up the street,
each one as vile as sin."

"Oh, *that's* who you were speaking of,"
I said as if entranced.
Gooseflesh on my forearms rose
when closer she advanced.

"You deem them most rambunctious?
Well, I guess I would agree.
But isn't that what mortal 'kids'
are all designed to be?"

"It was not *my* design,"
the striking woman muttered next.
"The fact that I must deal with them
at all does leave me vexed.

"But they were only customers
who came to see the zoo.
They left us just in time
and now my focus is on you.

"Ariadne's letter came last night
—a great surprise.
She told me of your trouble
and I can't believe my eyes.

"You, so young and handsome,
are the mighty Rowan Blaize?
The one who, through the ages,
never ceases to amaze?"

"Forgive if my appearance
at the moment underwhelms,"
I said to her while feeling
cast adrift in murky realms.

"Yet, if I stand before immortal
Circe of renown,
appearances would seem to be
deceiving all around."

She laughed at me, a sound like raindrops
striking silver bells.
How could this be the Mistress
of ten million vaunted spells?

"Your point is duly taken,"
she admitted with a smirk.
"Today, in fact, you find me
in the things I wear to work.

"It's all about an image, Rowan,
all about a task.
But let us go inside,
I know there's much you wish to ask.

"I'm closing down the place today
in honor of your visit.
We'll take a lovely tour.
That's not a problem, dear … or is it?"

"Quite alright," I muttered
as she led the way inside.
"Your company is welcome
after such a dreary ride."

"I saw your Aunt's old footman
drive you up, of course," she said.
"I can't believe she still employs
that morbid dunderhead."

"He has redeeming features,"
I responded with a sigh,
defending Bror, though at the time
I could not fathom why.

"I'm stunned to learn you dwell so close
to Auntie Addy's place.
Let's face it—potent witches
oft-prefer much greater space."

"Your Aunt and I are friends
from ancient days, as you may know.
Since I've been here we have not
chanced to meet, as schedules go."

Circe closed the massive doors
and locked them with a key.
Within, the great enclosure
was a feast for eyes to see.

Marble columns towered
to support a roof-topped entry.
A statue of Bastet beside a gate
nearby stood sentry.

Through this soaring archway
was an open-air preserve,
a row of gleaming cages filled
with beasts formed one great curve.

Bears and Bengal tigers lounged
near groups of wildebeest.
Gazelle and zebra grazed on dangling
grasses for their feast.

Llamas, goats, and one giraffe
were peeking through the bars.
A hippo in a wading pool
displayed great battle scars.

Wolves and badgers, chimps and pythons,
birds of every hue,
sat and stared, as if bereft
of other things to do.

No one else was in the place,
no mortal, imp, or elf.
"In case you wonder," Circe said,
"I run this place myself."

"You read my thoughts exactly,
Mistress. Now I see your plot.
I wondered what, in Pan's good name,
might bring you to this spot.

"But lest I am mistaken, here,
these sad and captive creatures,
once roamed rather freely
and they *all* had human features."

Circe laughed again—
the bells, the silver tinkling sound.
Her slender ivory fingers found
my neck and slipped around.

She brushed in playful passes
at my hair and gestured wide.
"I've changed them into what they've
always *been*, deep down inside.

"For any Greater Power knows that Man
is just a scourge.
Of course some won't admit it,
but we *all* have felt the urge …

" …to rid this world of every human—
fat and thin and tall.
To pulverize each mortal,
yes, the wise, the dim, the small.

"Oh, there are ways around the Deeper Laws,
to which I've warmed.
Ways like those you now behold …
the human state transformed."

"Circe, you have always walked the edge
and paid the price.
Like others you would rather fall
like lightning than think twice.

"With humankind we have no quarrel,
nor a cause to hate.
To persecute on principle
is surely tempting Fate.

"Quite frankly, I confess that humans
vex from time to time.
But just as often I have seen them
grasp for the sublime.

"Punishing a few of them
for crossing our designs,
or failing to adhere to their
sad path between-the-lines …

"… is well within our rights
but you of all should know by now
—the mindless war on humans
paints a curse upon your brow."

Circe slapped me hard upon the face
and laughed once more.
"You dare to lecture *me* when you
should grovel on the floor?

"And worse, dear boy, you didn't
even listen when I said
that I can show them mercy …
I don't *have* to see them dead.

"I see it in your spiteful eyes.
You think I'm playing games.
Like those I played in days gone-by
with more important names."

"Strike me all you wish, Fine Lady.
I will *not* condone
the spells that you are weaving here
on mortal flesh and bone.

"And since this is an ambush of some sort,
it's plain to see,
I, too, shall now dispense
with every form of courtesy.

"Was bad enough in ancient times,
when shipwrecked men you harmed.
How pitiful today that local *children*
be alarmed!

"You once ruled an island kingdom.
Now you run a zoo?
You once defeated warriors
that gods dispatched to you!

"I'm stunned that little group
that I saw leaving when I entered
are not this moment victims
of your 'Transformation Center.'

"I've seen some ruined wizards
and some sorcerers in hock,
but *never* did I think that such
a legend I would mock.

"And you deserve this ridicule,
O Circe great and cruel.
Alas, to think that you might heal
my illness—what a fool!

"Though moly may have broken me
and Auntie's lost her mind,
when faced with such a wretch as you
I *envy* humankind."

The Empress of All Witches
listened, patient, to my rant.
She smiled anew and spoke at last.
Her words flowed like a chant.

"First," she said, "there are so many
kinds of shipwrecked males.
The kind that I meet now
do not have use for oars and sails.

"Odysseus was a wondrous foe
and still has my respect.
An ape like him reminds us why
they learned to walk erect.

"But now the class of human
has declined to such a state
that very few among them
can be classified as 'great.'

"In fact, I've never seen a more
pathetic, weakened crop.
And when I think they can't get worse,
the madness doesn't stop.

"The billy-goat in cage fourteen
was once a drugged disgrace
who smashed a window in the night
and tried to rob my place.

"The hedgehog there in twelve was once
a drunken homeless hag
who littered my front doorway with
her shop-cart and her bag.

"That hippo with the slashed-up rump?
A well-known village glutton.
The aardvark, there, in number eight?
A rude old man from Sutton.

"You see, my Righteous Rowan,
how I do this world a favor?
Each mortal loser changed
is an accomplishment I savor.

"But this preserve is nothing.
Why, it's only just a start.
There *is* a greater plan in mind
in which you must take part."

"Oh, Circe, you're deluded.
I would *never* be of aid.
Your methods are deplorable,
and of the lowest grade."

"You have no choice, dear boy,"
she sniffed, and murmured a demand,
encircling me in white-hot rings
of power with her hand.

"There's something I must show you, Rowan.
Rise into the air.
It's time that you were introduced
to Circe's Face-Work Lair."

There was no thing that I could do
when gripped by such a force.
I hovered as she led me through
a long and winding course.

Past the awful cages
and the sullen beasts within,
she drew me deep into her world
as if hooked by the chin.

Down a flight of dripping, ancient steps
into a cave,
I followed mighty Circe
and was now her helpless slave.

Through all the way she said no word
until the cavern reached.
Her confidence controlled me
and my will her power leeched.

Descending in the darkness
I heard fingers as they snapped.
The torch-lit chamber came to life
with flames that swirled and flapped.

Before us stood an altar piled
with gobs of slimy crud,
and by the cave's rear wall
a bubbling pit of steamy mud.

Worse than any hellish pit,
to one foul wall were tethered
a host of gruesome face-masks
that were edged with blood and leathered.

Faces of all shapes that had been flayed
from many owners.
Seven foul, distorted mouths
that frowned like silent moaners.

Whither had she brought me
And what purpose could she crave,
deep within this catacomb,
this grim and putrid cave?

"Do not fret, young warlock,
I shall waste no further time
revealing my proposal, though,
I think *you'd* call it 'crime.'

"You are not here by accident—
on you I've kept my eye.
I've watched you now for fifty years,
on land, o'er sea, in sky.

"What manner of intrusion
is this tawdry revelation?"
I spat at grinning Circe,
who seemed pleased with my frustration.

"My plan to cull the human herd,
though noble it may be,
is one momentous task
that can't be done by only me.

"That's been the trouble, down through time,
with beings like ourselves.
We rarely seem to *organize*
like werebeasts … or like elves.

"Of course, upon occasion,
we can rally 'round a cause
and jettison the finest print
one finds in Deeper Laws.

"But sure enough, it never lasts,
for magic shuns a leader!
Unless you have a witch so strong
that *no one* can defeat her.

"Your Aunt knew all about it
on my island long ago,
but come the winters, interest waned
and off my maids would go.

"Behold, that island *and* this zoo
are models, nothing more.
They only hint at greater plans
I'm eager to explore.

"I need to spread my kingdom out,
extend my power-base.
And now I've found the answer
in the Magic of the Face!

"Imagine, Rowan, if you will,
The vision that I see—
the world's most mighty sorcerers
and *all* controlled by me.

"And that's where one like you comes in,
for few can match your skill.
Just think what I could do if I
could bend you to my will.

"The problem was your magic,
and it *had* to be curtailed …
at least until I had you in my grasp
and had prevailed.

"The moly that unhinged you
only days ago in Fez,
was planted by a man who always
does what Circe says."

"You base and evil wretch!" I cried.
"Twas *you* that brought me down!
I wish that I had fallen in the ocean,
there to drown."

"Yet that did not quite happen, Blaize.
I do my research well.
I knew that you were strong enough
to battle moly's spell.

"At least until you had arrived
or crashed on English soil.
And in this plan your Auntie,
Ariadne, played the foil!

"I knew that you were on your way
to London and her house.
I timed my efforts perfectly,
as furtive as a mouse.

"Your Aunt was asked for details
in the most off-handed way.
The fat old bat was willing
and she had a lot to say.

"With that, it was a matter
of logistics and a spell …
like making sure you found your way
to crusty old Narzell.

"Spying from a distance
is a method that I treasure.
For then I can manipulate
according to my pleasure."

"You even had that washed-up
Faery King in your employ?"
I roared at laughing Circe,
but, alas, I was her toy.

"He's really not a minion,
just a card I chose to play.
If you were not involved
I wouldn't give him time of day.

"The storm that dashed you earthward
was a little trick of mine,
and once you set out walking off
to London things were fine.

"I would have had you sooner
if that changeling of Narzell's
had minded her own business
and stayed clear of all my spells.

"But as it is, you made it
to your Auntie in due course.
The changeling, though, must pay.
She will be *lovely* as a horse.

"Leave that girl alone, you wicked thing!"
I fairly hissed.
"Miranda meant to help me,
one detail you clearly missed."

Circe shrugged and stood before
the wall of horrid faces.
"Now, it's time, my lad, when I
shall put you through your paces.

"The culmination of my plot
is seen in this display,
for you were not the *only* mage
to suffer Circe's Way.

"Seven faces peeled
from seven sorcerers of note.
All seven felled by moly
as it traveled down the throat.

"Each one of these I reeled-in like
a fish, as I reeled you,
and powerless before me
there was naught that they could do.

"Hecate was the first
and how ironic was her fate,
for she alone taught *me* the spell
I used to skin her pate!

"And there her face hangs lifeless
with some cord strung through the ears.
Beside her droops the mask of Merlin—
Oh! *He* shed some tears.

"The process was most painful
and perhaps to be regretted.
Those screams did not abate until
each face was fully shredded.

"But wait, there are five more
That you should 'meet' before we start.
Remember how I said that even *you*
will play your part?

"This is Doctor Faustus
and the next—Calypso fair.
And that is Baba Yaga,
plucked from icy Russian air.

"The next two are Cassandra
and sweet Morgan of the Fey,
who both were begging for their lives
once *I* got underway.

"It was a trifle gory, I admit,
but worth the mess.
I tried to reassure them that
their names I aimed to bless.

"For all of them shall live again
though modified they'll be,
their powers well-restored,
but now their wills belong to *me.*"

"You've changed into a demon, Circe,
morphed into a snake!
How can it be that such great Powers'
lives you blithely take?

"What black and midnight rituals
have left you so depraved?"
But Circe only cackled
as I ranted and I raved.

"The question you should ask, Young One,
is what I plan to do
with all these noble skins
and what shall *yet* become of you.

"For once they're resurrected
as my fine enchanted minions,
I'll have no need for puppet-strings,
for shackles, or for pinions.

"Instead these mighty agents will
disperse across the globe
and into mortal weaknesses
with magic they shall probe.

"Aye, if it takes a century
we'll bring the humans down,
leaving just the harmless,
most amusing ones around.

"Just think, it shall be better
than the gods have ever dreamed.
For Magic Folk shall have
the last dominion!" Circe screamed.

"Your warped, elitist nonsense
has a skewer running through it.
How could you think, O Circe,
that the earth will *let* you do it?

"Humankind has risen while
we've fallen for a reason.
Be still and cease this folly!
Be content with Magic's season!"

"Rowan, there's no way
I'm turning back upon this plan.
I will not fade or bow
to the machinery of Man.

"And you are wasting breath and time
protesting with such gall,
for notice there's an empty space
for one mask upon my wall.

"You do not think I'd miss the chance
To frighten and amaze
this prideful mortal world
without the help of Rowan Blaize?

"Indeed, my dear, you have a spot
in this grand gallery.
Despite your youth, so few can match
your hallowed pedigree.

"The powers you possess,
when not by allergy impaired,
are truly quite colossal
and with few can be compared.

"Then again your clan
is quite well known for magic brilliance,
for skill and ingenuity, for shrewdness
and resilience.

"Yet you, among them all,
have always been the true savant.
A talent like no other …
and that talent I now *want*.

"And lest you doubt that I can do
exactly as I say,
behold this 'demonstration mask'
I fashioned just today!"

Circe crossed the grim expanse
and reached behind the altar
I steeled myself and begged
the Elementals, lest I falter!

In her graceful hands she held
a blobby piece of flesh.
It dripped around the edges;
I could see the blood was fresh.

She spread it out before my eyes
on leather cords suspended—
The face of my Aunt Addy!
Her life most *clearly* ended!

"When Ariadne sent her letter
saying you'd come by,
I killed her postal gargoyle
and this morning I did fly ...

"… to pay old "Add" a visit
after you had left the place.
And with a Hydra's Claw
I brought her down and took her face!

"She will not figure in my plan,
but as a maid will do,
and best of all, till I have time,
she *can* take care of you."

Circe took the mask of doom
and to the altar turned.
The slimy pile of crud atop
now steamed as though it burned.

261

"The mud from my enchanted pool
I have infused with ichor.
I bled it out from Hades
long ago, with help from liquor.

"His shameful weakness was a boon
for one day I'd possess
the skill to animate all things
that death leaves in distress."

Circe shaped the formless lumps
of gruesome clay by hand
until she made the stinking thing
upon her altar stand.

She took the mask of murder,
tied it to her earthen tower,
and spoke in tongues forgotten
her most heinous words of power.

In the flicker of the cavern torchlight,
something fell had stirred.
The putrid slab of mud now seemed
to "hatch" as might a bird.

Undulating, writhing,
soon its color made a change.
The mask became a *part* of it
and then, by all that's strange …

… the thing took on a form
I recognized at once, with fear.
A "new" Aunt Ariadne,
only this one not so dear.

Circe wrapped it in a robe
she gathered from a chest.
The awful thing took gulping breaths
that heaved the ample breast.

"Speak, and I shall heed your voice,"
the "Anti-Addy" slurred
as Circe pointed at me with a
grim and vengeful word.

"Take the warlock Rowan Blaize,
and throw him in a cage.
I need a sharper Hydra claw
to skin *this* worthy mage."

The evil Auntie Addie grinned,
her eyes and teeth now black.
She slid down from the altar
and lurched forward in attack.

I shrank against the cavern wall
beneath a dangling face,
as Circe's Ariadne locked me
in a foul embrace.

Then as she dragged me up the steps,
below I heard a voice:
"At dawn I'll *own* you, Rowan Blaize,
you have no other choice."

IX

A Tardy God is Never Late, He's Always Just in Time ...

Broken and by beasts surrounded,
powerless, forever grounded,
caged by Circe's weird creation,
robbed of rescue, low of station,
at the gibbous moon I stare
through bars that mock my death-despair.
But lo! The thick of night surprises ...
Hermes, Fleet-of-Foot arises!

"Living things should not be caged,"
the god observed, uncaring.
A wand of special majesty
his perfect hand was bearing.

I sensed indifference in his voice
(the gods are all alike)
He said, "We hear that Circe plans
to skin you with a spike."

"A Hydra claw, to be exact,"
I muttered in the gloom.
"Feel free to come within and chat,
I *do* believe there's room."

Hermes touched the bars
and drew his hand back in distaste.
"I think that I shall stay outside.
There's little time to waste.

"A few of us got wind of this
unseemly plan she hatched.
Too bad for all the rest we learned
when you, old chap, were snatched."

"So now you're here to pity me
or rub my hardship in?
The love of gods for sorcerers
has ever been most thin."

"True enough," the whisper came.
His shadow waned and waxed.
"You must admit that, through the years,
our patience *has* been taxed.

"Yet that is not my real concern.
I'm here on Zeus' whim.
Cassandra was a friend of mine
and *quite* the friend to him.

"We heard she used the moly leaf
to wreck this latest crew.
Ironic, but at least the creature
thought of something new.

"In any case, great Zeus decrees
that *you* must have my wand
in honor of Cassandra—
My, he *really* was most fond.

"And here are tears from Aphrodite
gathered in a vial.
The only cure for moly,
so that ought to make you smile.

"Just drink them, you'll be fine again,
the magic back in action.
Although you're strong you'll need the wand
to truly give you traction.

"Circe is no picnic,
as I'm certain you deduced.
Employ your normal spells
and greater powers will be loosed.

"Even then, there is no guarantee
that you can beat her.
In fact, I must be going,
as I have *no wish* to meet her."

He handed me the vial
and his caduceus of gold.
I took them in bewilderment ...
such riches rare, untold!

"And all of this is due to some affair
that Zeus remembers?"
The eyes of Hermes glowed beyond
the bars like angry embers.

"Certain Ruling Powers in this world
and countless others,
do not care in the least if humankind
Old Circe smothers.

"My Master has his reasons
and I daresay they are just.
We're fading like you sorcerers,
for fade we surely must.

"Yet till we pass into the Void
that waits for All That Is,
a war for balance *must* be waged.
This war—Zeus feels it's his.

"We will not get involved beyond
the tokens you've been offered.
We will not render more advice
than that which has been proffered.

"But what about your wand?" I whispered.
"Don't you want it back?"
"That isn't my concern," said Hermes.
"Tend to the attack."

Amid the snoring animals
in cages all around.
The god just bowed his head
and lifted slowly from the ground.

He vanished in a flash
for that has always been his style.
Aghast, I gripped the wand
and then I drank the sacred vial.

X

Pardon My Caduceus

Circe in her Face-Work lair
was sharpening a claw
She'd pilfered from a Hydra
bound in chains, each snapping maw.

She glanced upon the faces
of the sorcerers she killed,
and relished every drop
of magic blood that she had spilled.

The boiling mud was ready
as the dawn announced the day.
Soon Rowan Blaize would be
a faceless corpse and thrown away.

The "zombie Ariadne"
had been sent to fetch the prize.
The Hydra claw was gleaming
when, to Circe's great surprise …

… a fearsome peal of thunder
shuddered down into the cave.
Her altar toppled over
in the sudden, jolting wave.

The masks upon the nearby wall
erupted into flame.
The mud-pool bubbled over
as a voice called out her name.

"Circe of the Lonely Island!
Daughter of the Sun!
Offspring of great Helios!
There's nowhere you can run!

"Summon all the magic
that you can—it won't avail you.
Bow down before the power
with which I shall now derail you!"

Rowan Blaize appeared
within the cave before his foe,
but *not* the Rowan Blaize
our Faithful Reader came to know.

A sorcerer without his magic
faces many trials.
But one who is *recharged* can cause
explosions heard for miles.

One like Rowan Blaize
can even do much greater things,
like take the forms of werewolves
armed with flaming dragon wings!

Yes, this is how our Blaize came down
to face the storied witch.
The staff of Hermes in his hand
and snapping like a switch.

The look on Circe's face was one
that turns most things to stone.
She quailed before recalling,
"I've a few tricks of my *own!*"

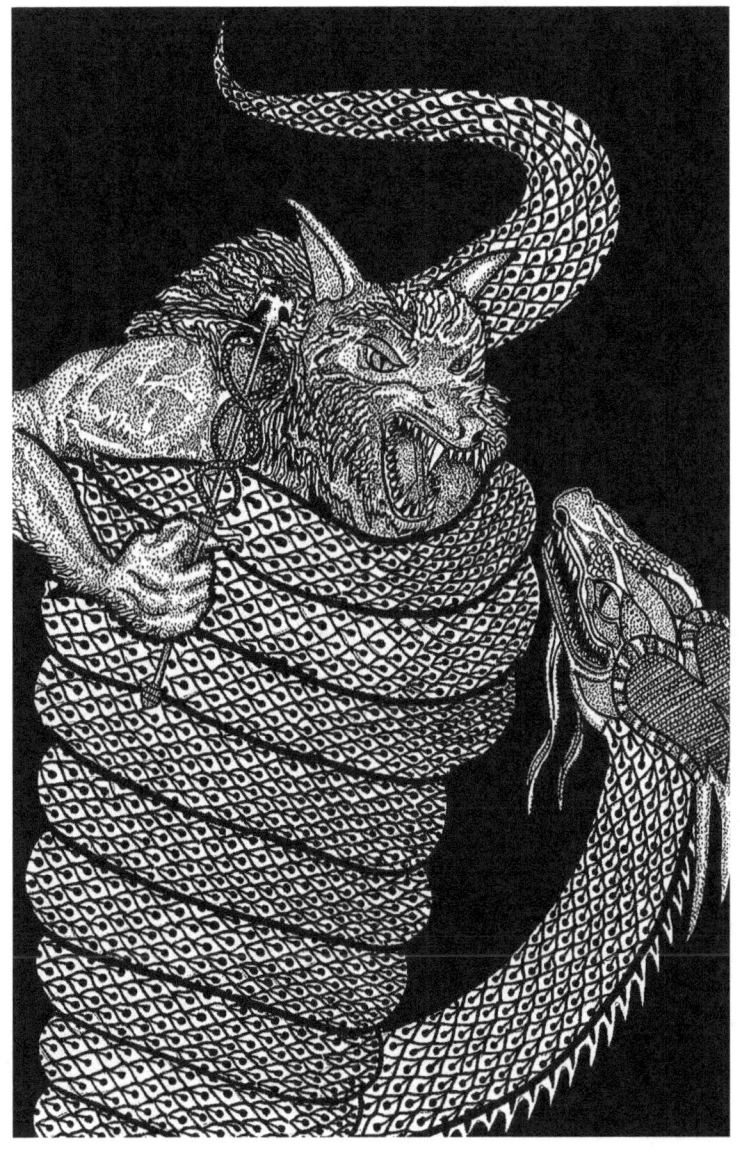

After all, she is the one
who made Charybdis roar.
She is the queen of Scylla,
who lurks on the ocean floor.

Shouting out a spell,
she turned herself into Behemoth.
Behold her razor fangs,
see how her breath with poison steameth!

They launched into each other
and they tore and scratched and slashed.
Throughout the whole of England
houses shook and lightning flashed.

Finally exhausted
and, with bloodied shredded flesh,
the two repelled each other
and their "monsters" came unmeshed.

Rowan crashed into a column.
Circe hit some shelves.
When both came-to, they saw that they'd
turned back into *themselves*.

They also saw the wand
that from dear Rowan's hand had spun.
It settled in a corner when their fight
at last was done.

Circe's eyes with hunger flared,
as Rowan spat and cursed.
She cackled, scrambling for the wand …

…But Rowan got there first.

EPILOGUE

Bror was quite beside himself.
His mistress had departed.
She'd clearly flown to parts unknown
and left him brokenhearted.

Within a week, the doorbell rang
and there stood Rowan Blaize.
"She's never coming back, dear Bror,
How *shall* you fill the days?"

Miranda, our good changeling
lounged upon a wall of stone,
when up to her a Mastiff lumbered,
chewing on a bone.

"Young lady, here's the dog you wanted.
Now, come follow me.
I have some things for you to draw …
It's time that you were free."

In Sutton's Art & Folk Museum,
there is a dusty nook
where hangs a framed old photo
on a slightly rusty hook.

All those who care to glance will see
a scene from country life …
A smiling farmer, Devon Mould,
and next to him, his wife.